The Shadow
of a
Mirage

A Tale of Ambition

BISWAJIT DAS

ISBN 979-8-89446-099-4

Dedicated to

This book is dedicated to all the dreamers who dare to dream big, and to the two beautiful women of my life, My mother and my wife, whose love and support fuel my dreams.

Disclaimer

All characters, events, and entities depicted in this novel are purely fictional and created for the purpose of entertainment. Any resemblance to actual persons, living or dead, or real-life events is purely coincidental. The views, opinions, and actions expressed by characters within this work are not reflective of any real individuals or organisations. This novel is a work of fiction, and any similarities to actual business entities, investment firms, or financial institutions are purely coincidental. The author does not endorse or promote any specific business practices or investment strategies depicted within this fictional narrative. Readers should interpret this work as a product of the author's imagination and enjoy it solely for its entertainment value.

Chapter 1

PROLOGUE

Another busy Monday morning, a police van carrying two young entrepreneurs rushed to the Bangalore High Court. It had been quite some time since the High Court accepted the PIL against Soriya Digitech Pvt. Ltd., a Bangalore-based IT consultancy firm founded by Aditya Chowdhury and Jayabrata Ganguly. They were now accused of cheating the youth of the country. Aditya, aka Adi, and Jayabrata, known as Joy, allegedly looted job seekers with false promises and established fake companies to run illegal businesses. The scam was estimated at around 60 crores over the last 4 years. The founders of the company, two young men, were arrested last week. It was their first trial court hearing.

The so-called scam of Soriya Digitech caused a lot of discussion and debate in the media. Nowadays, there's a big interest in startups and businesses in India. Slogans like 'Made in India' and 'Atmanirbhar Bharat' created massive hype among the youth to start their own businesses. Shows like Pitchers and Shark Tank also made people aware of the ins and outs of business.

However, this case was not straightforward; it had multiple layers, more than what was legal; the questions were about right and wrong, ethical or unethical, which provoked arguments between people, supporters, and people who didn't support it.

The Soriya Digitech case is a live example of the challenges one faces in finding the proper balance between ambition and ethics in business. Everyone wants to be successful, but that should not come at the price of honesty. The accusations against Adi and Joy made every young entrepreneur think about what's right and what's wrong in business.

Today, hundreds of curious eyes are glued to the news channels. The hearing was no longer limited to the interests of the founders or their company; it became the curiosity of every entrepreneurial spirit in the country. It was about what it meant to start a business in India, and regardless of the outcome, the story started redefining the testament of business in the country.

The police van slowly moved through the busy streets of the tech capital of India, making its way to the courthouse of justice. As they approached, A cluster of media and freelance reporters gathered eagerly to cover the prime-time story. Cameras flashed, questions flew, and excitement filled the atmosphere. Adi and Joy stepped out of the van, their expressions revealing a mix of feelings. Adi looked determined, while Joy seemed a bit anxious. They made their way through the crowd, surrounded by the police officers; each step of them was heavy with the weight of the uncertainty of the future.

An excited crowd gathered at one end of the packed corridor, carrying banners and messages, saluting Adi and Joy as modern-day heroes. They shouted enthusiastically, chanting "Adi-Joy Zindabad," drowning out the voices of nearby critics. Supporters passionately encouraged the duo for their brave initiative; they believed Adi and Joy had the potential to create jobs for the country's struggling youths in the tech-driven market.

A group of angry individuals gathered on the other side of the corridor. They were holding posters in their hands that stated, "Breaking laws must have consequences." One poster boldly said, "Cheaters Deserve Punishment." The environment was heated, with a mix of respect and hatred, showing the struggle of the city to take a clear side.

Despite the ongoing uncertainty and anxiety, Adi and Joy remained strong and prepared to face whatever challenges lay ahead.

They entered the courtroom; the imposing doors swung open to welcome them inside. On the inner side of the bustling room, papers shuffled, and voices murmured, creating a busy atmosphere. Despite the serious ambience, everyone was fully focused and energised. In the front, the judge's chair emanates authority and gravitas, while outside, the faint sounds of the city seep in, enhancing the scene's ambience. It was a snapshot frozen in time, where anticipation and tension intermingled, and the trial's outcome swung on a knife's edge.

The trial started exactly at 10 a.m., and within no time, it became evident that both the prosecution and the defence needed to exert their utmost effort to prove their points.

Outside, the once-lively crowd fell silent. It was like the entire city held its breath. The opening statement came up, leaving Adi and Joy's fate a mystery. The moment was filled with emotion and suspense. The city of Bangalore, too, matched its rhythm with Adi and Joy, eagerly awaiting what would happen next.

Adi started feeling the weight of the moment pulling him down. His thoughts about their dream, plan, and ongoing consequences started racing through his mind, intensifying the pressure on him. It was getting difficult for him to maintain his composure as the tension grew with each passing moment.

Despite his inner turmoil, he tried to appear confident and composed as much as possible, but inside, doubts and fears were stabbing him continuously. Every word from the prosecutor felt like a blow, pushing him to think quickly about how to defend himself.

The courtroom seemed like a battleground to Adi. He was observing every detail attentively and tried to anticipate the possible direction in which the trial could go.

Adi couldn't resist thinking about Joy and how he was coping with the situation. He knew it was too much for Joy to handle. Joy was a techie and, by heart, an artist; he had never been as fearless as he needed to be now. Adi was the one whom he had trusted before jumping into this ocean. And today, Adi felt responsible for Joy's pain.

Even though the evidence against them was piling up, Adi was not ready to give up. He held a tiny ray of optimism in his heart, despite the feeling that everything was going against them. But with every passing moment, it became increasingly difficult to hold on to hope.

Standing side by side, Adi and Joy showed silent support for each other. However, they were fighting their own battles inside. Adi looked determined outside, yet beneath the surface, a tornado of fear and guilt churned within him. On the other hand, Joy looked troubled, clearly affected by the serious accusations against them. Joy, who used to be full of energy, now seemed withered by the gravity of the situation.

Adi looked at Joy, and his guilt increased at the sight of his best friend's fearful face. They had been through a lot together, but now their friendship was going through its biggest challenge, being the poster boys of a national scandal.

The prosecutor continued presenting his argument on the case, and the courtroom transformed into a battleground of facts and allegations. Each piece of evidence he presented was like a nail in the coffin for Adi and Joy, establishing the scam they were accused of. Adi felt like all eyes were on him, judging his every move. Even though he tried to ignore them, he couldn't shake the feeling of doubt.

When the prosecution finished the argument, it was the turn of the defence. The response was ready and well-calculated. Each argument was carefully designed with detail and logic to dismiss the prosecution's theory.

As the trial progressed, Adi lost sight of the journey up to this point. He recalled the early days, filled with excitement, innovation, and ambitious goals. They started their adventure with the objective of transforming the technology sector and making a positive impact on the world. However, facing the harsh reality of the courtroom, their once dazzling vision became tainted by doubt and sorrow.

In those moments of reminiscing, Adi was shaken by the heavy voice of the defence. "I object!" exclaimed Manjunath, their lawyer, his voice resolute and unwavering. It was a reminder that, no matter how deep they were, they still had a chance to fight. As the courtroom erupted into a flurry of activity, Adi felt a glimmer of hope ignited within him. It reminded Adi and Joy that no matter how terrible the situation was, there was always a ray of light in the darkness.

With a determined stance, Manjunath kept his debate ongoing. He was an experienced lawyer. His voice reflected the confidence of his expertise. With a conviction, he declared, "This case has no foundation, absolutely none!" His words resonated through the courtroom, bringing back confidence for Adi and Joy.

Manjunath kept defending his clients. He said, "Soriya Digitech, owned by Mr. Aditya and Joyabrata, never cheated anyone out of money." He stressed how the company had created job opportunities for many over the past 4 years, employing numerous students who were overlooked by larger corporations.

As he spoke, Manjunath's eyes fixed on the honourable judge, hoping to convey his message. "Our world is moving towards digitalisation every day. Jobs are being created, but traditional ones are getting replaced by automation. Even the demand for private tutors is decreasing due to AI tools and online classes."

Manjunath's argument gained strength with each of his words. He was confident and determined in his voice to prove that his clients were innocent. The lawyer told the court a story about the changing world with the flow of technology. He talked about Aditya and Joyabrata, who saw an opportunity to help students, especially those who weren't studying technology. They created opportunities for those students and gave them a fair chance. They recruited them and helped them grow as techies. He made it sound like Aditya and Joyabrata were the first ones to do this. "My client took the mission to provide everyone at least a chance to learn and make a position in the world of software and technology, not just people who studied engineering."

Manjunath's narrative gained momentum over time, emphasising Aditya and Joyabrata and their company, Soriya Digitech, as a gift for middle-class students. In his words, "It's a tale of empowerment, a tale of breaking down the barriers and levelling the field of an industry that is often dominated by the privileged."

The argument of the defence lawyer created a huge impact in the courtroom. It forced the critics to reconsider their opinions. Some of them agreed with Manjunath's argument, while others looked worried and were not fully convinced.

Manjunath continued to address the court; his eyes were confident, and his voice carried a touch of personal conviction. He spoke not just as a legal representative but as a believer in his client's cause. "My clients are not criminals," he asserted firmly, "they are visionaries who saw a gap in the system and dared to fill it. They are not greedy; they believe in inclusivity and providing opportunities to others. It was never the greed of fortune that motivated them, but a genuine desire to make a positive impact on the world around them."

In his closing statement, Manjunath requested the Court of Justice not to punish innovation but to appreciate it. He also requested to look beyond the surface to see the larger picture and recognise the potential for good that lay within his clients' endeavours. It was an appeal for compassion and justice. The courtroom fell silent with the closure of the defence. The echoes of Manjunath's words remained in the air, giving a feeling of hope even though no one knew what would happen in the trial.

The prosecution quickly countered Manjunath's speech with many objections, turning the courtroom into a battleground again, where both sides fought for their points. In the objections, the opposing side stressed the large sum of money involved; in all these, they argued that starting such a big company needed a lot of money. Raised concern about Soriya Digitech's integrity and source of funding.

In the chaos of the arguments, Adi's eyes found comfort in Tanya's calming presence among the worried faces in the crowd. Her calm face was like a lighthouse in a stormy sea. When their eyes met, it felt like they were speaking without words, silently promising to support each other no matter what.

At that moment, the noise of the courtroom faded away, leaving just Adi and Tanya in their own world. While the legal battle was ongoing, their silent exchange became a safe haven, a place of quiet reassurance far from the chaos. Tanya's support was like a lifeline for Adi. It always reminded him that he wasn't alone in this storm. Even when the blame was everywhere and the tensions were high, the connection between Adi and Tanya grew stronger. Their connection was like a powerhouse, which supplied Adi with the strength to face the uncertainties.

The courtroom fell silent for a moment as the judge was about to deliver his comment for the day and share his judgement on the bail application. After hearing from both sides, he announced his decision that "the bail application for Aditya and Joyabrata is granted." The judgement had certain conditions that they must follow.

"The accused are required to cooperate with the Enforcement Directorate in the investigation and help the officers with all the necessary documents and records of the company for the last 4 years," the judge added. "Aditya and Joyabrata are prohibited from leaving the country without prior permission from the court. Additionally, they must report daily to the local police station until the final verdict is delivered." The court concluded the proceedings for the day with the judgement. The next hearing was scheduled for one month from today.

Adi and Joy felt a bit relaxed with the grant of the bail. Adi hugged Joy to comfort him and whispered to his ears, "Don't worry, I'll handle everything. We're businessmen, and this is just part of our journey."

Joy smiled a little and replied quietly, "I'm sorry, Adi, but I never wanted to be a shameless businessman."

The courtroom drama finished for the day, spreading a complex wave of emotions, with moments of relief, uncertainty, and friendship tested during the legal battle.

That night was quite heavy for Adi. He was burdened by conflicting emotions. Getting the bail was a small victory in the midst of legal turmoil, but the echo of Joy's words vibrated relentlessly in his mind. "I never wanted to be a shameless businessman." Joy's words started haunting him, creating doubt on the path they both had chosen.

Adi lay awake in the quiet solitude of the bedroom, staring into the darkness as his thoughts churned. He couldn't throw away the feeling that was biting him from inside. The question was the choice of path that had led him and Joy to this point. The ambitious plans they had made now seemed tainted by the shadow of legal scrutiny.

Tanya's presence next to him offered a sense of comfort. Her gentle touch and caring words provided a brief respite from the storm raging within Adi. She suggested that he could stay over at her place tonight. Adi agreed to that without any hesitation. He knew he needed Tanya with him now to function; he could not manage alone in this situation.

Tanya was a true friend, and she could never leave Adi alone in this circumstance. The peace they found in the stillness of the night was shattered by a sudden ring of Adi's phone. His heart skipped a beat as he reached for it, the caller's ID revealing Anish's name. With a sense of foreboding, Adi answered the call, sensing that something was not right.

"Hello, Anish," Adi said.

Anish's voice was fumbling. "I found Joy wrapped in blood on the floor of his room. I brought him to the hospital. Please come, Adi, as early as possible." He said.

The news pulled the ground under his feet. His hand started trembling while his mind started rushing, anticipating many possibilities. In an instant, the complexities of life faded in importance compared to the well-being of his closest friend and business partner, knowing that he needed to be there immediately.

The sudden surprise turned the lazy night into a rush hour. It reminded Adi that the difficulties were far from over.

Chapter 2

THE FIRST MEET

Bangalore, the "Silicon Valley of India," is known for its warmth and innovation. It's a place where dreams meet innovation and ideas take flight. The city is famous for its pleasant weather, modern tech parks, and vibrant nightlife. Bangalore has the largest number of tech parks in India, where millions of people come to work from all over the world.

The city is located in the heart of southern India, and its strategic location plays a major role in its rapid growth. Bangalore also owns the title of "garden city," with a significant number of lakes and gardens. The city is surrounded by perfect weekend getaways. In the west lies Western Ghat mountain ranges, while in the southwest, the majestic town of Mysore, and further on, the 'Queen of the Hills,' Ooty. Towards the northwest, there's the home of the beautiful sea beaches of Mangalore, Udupi, Gokarna, and many more. At the east stands the holy temple for pilgrimage, Tirumala Tirupati, Horsley Hills, and further, the coastal town Pondicherry, to name just a few.

With its picture-perfect buildings, bustling streets, and vibrant markets, Bangalore offers a standard quality of life with the opportunity to fly high. It is a melting pot of cultures, with people from all over the country and even from outside of India united by their dreams.

But, Bangalore's journey to becoming a global tech hub was not an overnight success. It began decades ago, at a time when the city was little more than a quiet cantonment town under British rule. Back then, it was known for its pleasant weather and green surroundings. However, things changed when Hindustan Aeronautics Limited (HAL) was established in 1940. This marked the beginning of Bangalore's ascent to becoming a prominent name in the world of technology.

After India's independence, Bangalore became a favourite destination for companies due to its strategic location and skilled workforce. The Indian Institute of Science (IISc) was established here in 1953 and, in no time, became one of India's top research centres. In the 1970s and 1980s, more companies, both local and international, started investing in Bangalore, especially in aerospace, defence, and electronics. With the economy opening up in the early 1990s, Bangalore saw further growth. The city's first software park, the International Tech Park, Bangalore (ITPB), opened in 1994.

However, Bangalore started to make its mark on the global map in the late 1990s and early 2000s, when there was a global IT explosion due to the Y2K issue and the dot-com boom. It created a huge demand for software services. Big companies like Infosys, Wipro, and Tata Consultancy Services (TCS) became key players, making Bangalore a top spot for outsourcing work. Bangalore has always kept its focus on encouraging creativity and new ideas, securing its lasting place in the world of technology. On average, approximately 22 startups register here every month, along with the growth of larger organisations.

It is not only the technology and innovation; this city has a jolly soul to it and knows how to celebrate life. As night falls, Bangalore lights up with its vibrant nightlife. Endless parties and fun-filled gatherings in the clubs and pubs make the scene lively. The city bagged the title of the Pub Capital of India, with a high number of pubs and clubs.

However, after enjoying a drink, sometimes it becomes hectic to find a taxi back home. Though the techies are good at using mobile applications to book a cab, it's up to the driver to offer the ride or simply cancel it. The cancellation might come most of the time. The relationship with the cab services is like finding a partner for a single soul; keep trying without getting demoralised by the rejections.

In this city of surprises, where technology and innovation bond with life, each day unfolds like a comedy skit, with Bangalore as the charismatic star. So, get ready, or better yet, treat yourself to a delicious dosa as we embark on an unpredictable journey through Silicon Valley's very own sitcom – welcome to Namma Bengaluru!

Bangalore treats the newcomers to a journey of challenges, which helps to build resilience for these newbies who just came out of their hives. Adapting to the city's frenetic pace isn't easy. Everyone strives to find their own way in this competitive environment. Getting a job and making a name in the industry is really a rollercoaster journey of ambition and determination.

Despite all the challenges, Bangalore welcomes everyone with open arms. Each year, fresh graduates from across the country pack their bags and move to Bangalore in search of fortune. Some are armed with job offers, while others are fuelled solely by hope. All of them have one thing in common: a desire to leave their imprint on the technological landscape.

The city is flooded with young professionals, and as an obvious result, the crowd sparked a rise in housing demand, leading to the rise of Bangalore's PG (paying guest) culture. Imagine yourself walking through narrow streets or busy roads, each filled with PG accommodations. These temporary accommodations offer shelter for the new arrivals. They're similar to dormitories, where residents become close, forming lasting friendships while sharing rooms and enjoying life together, overcoming challenges along the way.

You'll find a blend of various room arrangements in these PGs. Some are simple and pocket-friendly, quite similar to army barracks with bunker beds and bare minimal facilities. Then there are the executive ones, where luxury is the top priority. These executive luxury accommodations offer private rooms with all the modern amenities of a star hotel. Sometimes, these accommodations even go far in their offerings, with a swimming pool, clubhouse, gymnasium, and many more.

Anyway, regardless of the size or facilities of the PG accommodations, they play a crucial role in Bangalore's vista, offering a safe haven to the newcomers in the middle of the city's hustle and bustle. In addition to convenient living arrangements, PGs also provide the opportunity to learn openness, acceptance, and sharing while living here as a community.

Adi and Joy's unexpected encounter occurred in one of the PGs called "Happy PG" in Mahadevapura. Madhu Reddy, a friendly, welcoming middle-aged Telugu man, was the owner and manager of the PG.

The PG was strategically located between the 2 major lifelines of the eastern part of the city: Outer Ring Road and Whitefield Main Road. "Happy PG" Stood as an oasis in the middle of the city's perpetual motion. The best part about the location was the easy access to get around, whether by hopping on a train at K. R. Puram station, exploring the busy Marathahalli area, or even travelling to the IT parks in Whitefield. Close to the PG, there were two huge shopping spots: the Phoenix Market City Mall and the VR Mall. They were always buzzing with excitement! Those places remained lively on weekends, with plenty of cool pubs, bars, and shopping adventures, making it a perfect night-out spot with friends.

The six-story building of the Happy PG was not only a place to stay; it was a rich fabric interwoven with elements like brotherhood, fight, late-night adda (chats), and stories of weekend adventures. Stepping onto the ground floor of PG felt like entering a busy market filled with energy and companionship. During the day, the ground floor served as a parking space for motorcycles, but in the morning or at night, it transformed into a lively dining area where residents got together for meals. However, punctuality was very important there, as the latecomers might miss out on the best menus. The foods were limited as per headcount, and boiled eggs for breakfast or sweets for dinner were usually the first items to get over.

In Happy PG, the typical day starts with breakfast at 7 am, and dinner is served exactly at 8 pm, marking the end of a busy day filled with work and fun. During weekends, Happy PG offers a special lunch menu and the residents eagerly gather in the dining area for the exotic weekend meal. The dining area was the clubhouse of this simple PG accommodation, where residents come together to enjoy meals, laughter, and chatter.

Happy PG transcends being merely a place to rest; it's a thriving community where friendships blossom, meals are shared, and lasting memories are made. Situated in the heart of Bangalore, it serves as a launchpad for new adventures and city exploration, offering residents a home away from home amidst the urban hustle.

The rooms at Happy PG resembled typical two- or three-bedroom apartments. The master bedrooms were shared by two individuals, with an attached bathroom. The dormitory rooms accommodate 3 to 4 occupants. Even the kitchen had been converted into a single room, offering a bit of privacy for an extra fee. On each of the floors, a mini-community formed here, creating interesting stories of friendship and more. It felt similar to the college hostel wings; each floor had its own distinct way of fostering brotherhood or occasional conflicts with neighbouring floors.

Today, Adi received his first paycheck and decided to throw a party to celebrate - it was his first salary, after all. He had been enjoying a two-sharing room all to himself until now, and it had become a gathering spot for everyone in the PG.

Room no 303 was filled with cigarette smoke, and the strong scent of Old Monk rum mingled with the sounds of laughter and bonding. As the clock inched closer to 8 pm, there was a knock on the door, disrupting Adi's celebration. Madhu Reddy, the owner, was at the door with a serious expression. He scanned the room, taking note of the smoke and the jovial atmosphere.

With a blend of sternness and warmth in his tone, Madhu addressed Adi and the others, "How many times do I have to remind you – this isn't a chimney! If you need to smoke, go outside, enjoy your smoke, and then come back."

Adi was not ready to let anything ruin his happiness today. He replied, "Anna, it's my first payday! It's just me and the third-floor group here; no one else, no trouble. We promise!"

Madhu understood that the evening would get wild, so he chose not to stretch the topic. He smiled and introduced Joy.

"So, here is your new roommate; he will share this room with you, Adi."

The unexpected guest joined Adi's celebration. At first, it was a surprise in the middle of the party. Adi then thought It was payday after all - maybe Joy's sudden arrival meant good luck in his financial journey.

Joy was warmly welcomed. Suddenly, there was another knock on the door. It was Madhu again, this time with a smile on his face. As Adi opened the door, Madhu whispered with a twinkle in his eye, "Save some fun for me. I'll join the party once my wife goes to bed." Adi smiled and nodded in agreement. "Sari Anna" (Alright, Brother)

The room echoed with laughter, glasses clinking, and a welcoming atmosphere as Joy joined the group. Although a bit shy, Joy had a good sense of humour and quickly became part of the cheerful bunch. Anish, the youngest member there, was particularly loved for his innocent and sometimes quirky behaviour. He shared the dormitory with two lively folks – Jumbo, Shukla bhaiya, who was like a mature figure, and Kesarilal, also known as Sambhu the most desi among them. They all warmly embraced Joy into their circle.

In a gesture of friendship, Anish offered a drink to the new roommate.

Anish: "Hey Joy, buddy! Welcome to the madness. Your first day at Happy PG deserves a celebration. Here, have a drink."

Joy felt a bit uneasy initially, but with a glimmer in his eyes, he took the glass.

Joy: "Well, when in Bangalore, right? Cheers!"

With time, laughter filled the room, the atmosphere was tipsy, and the clock crept towards midnight, with the bottle of spirits slowly depleting. Eventually, they realised that the bottles were empty; they ran out of drinks and needed more.

Kesarilal spoke out with a garbled sound, his mouth full of gutkha (betel nuts). "Adi, my friend, can you please bring last week's bottle from our room?"

But Shukla bhaiya reminded the reality that Kesarilal had already finished the bottle alone last night after the fight with his distant love.

Shukla said sarcastically, "Beta Kesari, that bottle is history from last night. We are out of stock. We need to go out."

The need for more drinks set the stage for a midnight adventure, and as always, Adi became the promoter of this tipsy tale.

Adi was always ready for these types of night events, but he threw in a condition,

Adi: "Alright, folks! I'm up for the challenge, but I'm not going alone. Someone has to be my partner in crime."

After a brief and detailed discussion lasting 15 minutes, the group finally reached a conclusion: it was Joy's first day, and he seemed relatively sober. Thus, the responsibility of acquiring the tonic fell on Adi and his newfound companion, Joy.

Anish: "Joy, buddy, enjoy! Tonight's your introduction to our crazy adventures. Are you ready for a night-out in Bangalore?"

Joy smiled shyly as a new guy to the group,

"Why not? Let's get some experience!"

They made their way through the night, sneaking down the stairs. And then jumped over the wall to avoid the locked main door – a secret mission of midnight alcohol quest began.

❖ ❖ ❖

The main door of the PG closes at 12 a.m. in the night. It was not allowed to go out or in after that. Adi whispered to Joy, "Let's be careful, buddy. Follow me, and we'll be back before anyone notices."

Their bike (motorcycle) was intentionally parked outside, as it was quite anticipated that they might need to go out at night in search of liquor. They started the engine and rode into the quiet night. Both were excited and enjoying the night ride. It was like a pleasant feeling of doing something crazy for these recent graduates. The memory and creativity of their college days still have not completely faded.

Adi knew the risks of going out for alcohol late at night, so he found a quiet place to park the bike, just a lane away from the main road that led to the liquor shop, which was only 100 metres away from there.

Adi suggested, "Let's walk from here."

Joy asked, "Why?"

Adi explained, "It's the main road, buddy. The police might come, and we're both drunk, plus we're not wearing helmets."

Joy nodded, "That's not a good idea. We shouldn't drink and drive, especially without helmets and in our boxers."

Adi thought of a solution, "You're right. When I have enough money, I'll start a liquor delivery company, especially for weekends and midnights."

"And cigarettes, too," Joy added.

They walked towards the shop, continuing their discussion on the unique business idea. Suddenly, a police van pulled up in front of the store. Adi sensed trouble and stopped Joy.

Adi said urgently, "Joy, let's run. I guess the police are raiding the shop."

Without asking any questions, Joy turned around, and the two of them ran back to the bike without a pause. As they reached, they took deep breaths to calm down the heart, and then they lit a cigarette.

Joy was confused; he asked, "Why did we run? We haven't even reached the store yet."

Adi shrugged. "Who knows? In moments like these, my brain just says, 'Run.' I can't explain it, but it feels like the right thing to do."

Joy chuckled at the situation.

Now, Adi had another problem: they couldn't return to the PG empty-handed; it was against the PG rules. But where were they going to get liquor in the middle of the night?

Joy then helped with an idea. He suggested riding through the inner narrow lanes to reach the other side of the PG, the Outer Ring Road. And then the plan was to find someone who looked intoxicated because, as the saying goes, only a fellow drunk knows where to find alcohol.

The quest of a drunkard started, and finally, they spotted a man stumbling on the street. He was clearly showing signs of tipsiness. Adi stopped the bike next to him and asked, "Excuse me, where can I buy some alcohol?"

The man looked surprised and replied, "Do I look like a walking bar to you?"

Joy understood the mistake and explained politely, "No, sir, we're sorry. We were just hoping you might know where to find some liquor. It's my friend's birthday today, but it seems like all the shops are closed. So, we thought maybe you could help us."

Adi sweetened the deal: "And if you help us, we can offer you a quarter of alcohol as thanks to your greatness."

The man became excited with the offer: "A quarter? Well, then, I can definitely help. Let me hop on your bike."

With the man guiding them, Adi drove towards a store nearby, but when they arrived, it was closed. But the man seemed like a pro and didn't give up. He knocked on the shutter and asked for one full and one-quarter bottle of Old Monk.

The shopkeeper, on the other hand, was cautious but eager to make some additional money. He asked for the money first. Adi paid him. He took the money and closed the shutter. After 5 minutes of silence, it looked like the shutter would never lift again. But it was not the case; the shutter lifted slightly again, and a hand passed out a packet containing a full and a quarter bottle of alcohol.

The drunk man snagged the packet and immediately took out the quarter bottle. He then handed over another bottle to Adi and requested a favour: a ride to the bus stop.

Adi and Joy, now partners in this late-night adventure, agreed to the request. They dropped the man off at the bus stop and rode back to the PG with their precious bottle. They felt a sense of accomplishment and excitement. Their mission was a success, and now the night's celebration could continue.

That night destiny started writing a tale of friendship, without the knowledge of these two young souls. The tale, which will eventually drive them to the land of dreams fuelled by ambition.

Chapter 3

RAJA YA PRAJA

Adi and Tanya rushed towards the hospital as soon as they received the news of Joy's hospitalisation.

Adi drove as fast as possible to the hospital with Tanya by his side, both worried about Joy. The streets at midnight were quite empty; only a few trucks were crossing the city in the absence of the traffic. The silence of the night was being disrupted by the sound of Adi's racing heart, audible under the moonlight. They were heading to Oasis Hospital in Whitefield, where Joy was admitted.

As Adi and Tanya arrived at the hospital, the seriousness of the situation hit them hard. Anish stood there alone, looking worried under the bright light of the hospital entrance. Adi felt a pang of pain in his chest as he rushed to Anish. The air felt thick, making it hard to breathe with their shared concern about what might happen next.

Outside, the night covered the world in darkness. A few streetlights were barely lighting the empty sidewalk. The parking lot, usually full, now sat in complete silence, with only a few cars scattered around. Their shadows blended into the darkness, deepening the feeling of emptiness at night. The world was nearly motionless; only occasional passersby, perhaps late-night workers, or lost souls broke the silence with their hurried footsteps. Their presence was fleeting, a mere whisper in the vast expanse of the night.

Against this backdrop of stillness and silence, the hospital building loomed tall and steadfast. Soft light spilt from its windows, casting gentle rays into the night. The building almost seemed to breathe, with medical staff tirelessly working inside.

Meanwhile, a tense group gathered outside the hospital, their faces drawn with worry and anticipation. They were waiting with heavy hearts for an update on their loved one inside. Their expressions displayed the anxiety they felt; each breath held in anticipation, every prayer hoping for a swift resolution to their trouble.

Adi parked the car and ran to Anish. He was breathless and anxious, desperate to know about Joy's condition. "Anish! What happened? How is he?" Adi's voice trembled with worry.

Anish shook his head with a fearful face. "I don't know, Adi. I was in my room."

Sensing the urgency, Tanya attempted to calm the situation. "Let's find out how he is first. We can discuss the details later. Where is he?"

The three rushed through the hospital corridors, their footsteps echoing their worried hearts. Anish guided them to the intensive care unit where Joy lay, his life depending on the machines and monitors.

Anish pointed to a closed glass door with a serious look. "He's in there, Adi."

Adi reached the door with dizzy steps. He gathered all his courage and tried to open the door, but it was locked. Inside, Joy was lying still, connected to tubes and wires. The visual through the glass was more disturbing for Adi. He looked at his friend's pale face. It was so different from the lively person he knew.

Tanya stood beside him, holding his hand quietly, supporting him in this catastrophe of life. "Joy... what happened?" Adi's voice came out involuntarily.

Anish was breathing out heavily. He tried to explain the situation to the best of his knowledge. "It was around 11.30 p.m. when I heard a heavy sound; initially, I ignored it but later thought to check. I checked the living room and the kitchen but couldn't find any source, so I thought of knocking on Joy's room. The door was closed but not locked. I opened it and found him unconscious on the floor, covered in blood. I don't know, Adi. It all happened so suddenly. But I believe he fell down, and the corner of the table hit his head, causing the injury."

Tanya gently placed her hand on Adi's shoulder and said, "Let's talk to the doctors." Adi nodded, torn with fear.

The hospital room, usually a place of healing, felt heavy with silent prayers for their friend's recovery. They hurried to the doctor's room. Adi's mind was filled with worries and anxiety.

He nervously asked the doctor about his friend's condition.

Adi: "How's he doing, doctor? What happened?"

The doctor paused for a moment before responding.

Doctor: "Excuse me."

Adi clarified, "I'm Aditya Chowdhury, Joyabrata's friend. He's in the ICU."

The doctor now recognised him, replied with compassion: "Mr Chowdhury, your friend suffered a serious injury to the back of his head. There's been significant bleeding, so surgery is necessary to address it. And one thing he was severely intoxicated when this happened. He might have drunk too much alcohol."

Adi's face reflected his fear and concern: "Surgery? Is everything alright? Anything serious?"

The doctor tried to reassure him, "We're doing everything possible. The surgery is needed to stop the bleeding and prevent further damage. It's scheduled for tomorrow morning."

Adi, gripping the table next to him, "Can I see him?"

Doctor: "Of course, but keep it brief. He needs to rest."

Adi approached Joy's bed in the ICU. He was surrounded by several tubes and monitors, which might help him stay alive. Time froze for Adi as he stepped into the sterile room. The antiseptic smell and the hum of machines intensified Adi's growing sense of panic.

A wave of numbness washed over Adi. Seeing Joy hooked up to machines, the steady beeping of monitors, and his friend's pale face filled Adi with deep sorrow and helplessness. It was not the same joy he knew, highlighting how fragile life could be. It just takes a moment to change everything.

Joy's condition hit Adi very hard, leaving him feeling lost and unable to understand what to do next. With a heavy heart, he stepped out of the room and walked silently towards the exit gate. Outside, the quiet of Whitfield Road surrounded him, magnifying the emptiness he was feeling inside. Tanya, understanding his need for comfort, followed him silently; her presence was always a silent reassurance for Adi in the middle of the uncertainty.

The deliberately quiet atmosphere seemed to accuse Adi, with each step on the deserted road a reminder of his perceived culpability in the unfolding tragedy. He lit up a cigarette for a little comfort, its glow creating shadows on his troubled face. His voice trembled with self-blame and regret as he spoke.

"If anything happened to Joy, I'd never forgive myself. I don't know how I will face his father. He's already going through so much pain, and I can't bear to add to it."

His words hung in the air, a solemn reflection of the guilt and anguish consuming him after Joy's accident.

Tanya sensed Adi's inner turmoil. She took the cigarette from his hand and responded after a deep puff.

"Adi, I might not be your girlfriend, but I care about you. You're a good man, and as far as I know, you'd never intentionally hurt anyone. You're strong, strategic, and realistic. Blaming yourself isn't what you are. I know wiping your tears won't change anything; instead, I can only say, please stay strong and face this head-on. Do not blame yourself; that won't fix anything; it'll only make things worse."

Her words, accompanied by another puff of smoke, carried a blend of comfort and conviction, an attempt to anchor Adi in the storm that threatened to overwhelm him.

Suddenly, Adi's phone broke the tense silence of the night, disrupting his conversation with Tanya. Diya's name lit up the screen, and Adi paused for a second to calm down before picking up.

Adi: "Hello."

Diya's voice, frantic and worried, spilt through the phone.

"Adi, Anish tried to call me and then sent a text message about taking Joy to the hospital. What happened?"

Adi tried to choose his words carefully and replied,

"Diya, Joy had a bit too much to drink. He fell in his room and got hurt. We're at Oasis Hospital in Whitefield. If you want, I can pick you up here."

Diya tried to avoid the details and asked, "How is he doing now?"

Adi assured her, "He's fine. Tell me, did you guys have a fight?"

Diya hesitated before responding, "It's complicated. I wanted to break up with him. It's tough for me, Adi, after all this police and court drama. But trust me, I want him to be safe. I love him."

Adi was surprised by Diya's words; he thought for a moment and replied, "Don't worry, Diya. I get it. Get ready; I'll come to get you here."

Diya, hesitatingly, questioned, "But Adi?"

Adi, with a heavy heart, said, "Joy is in the ICU. The doctors will operate on him in a few hours."

Silence on the other end of the line spoke volumes, only broken by the sound of Diya's tears. Adi turned to Tanya and said, "Tanya and I are coming. Get ready."

Tanya nodded with understanding and said, "I'll check on Anish. I'll join you in the car."

Tanya walked into the hospital to tell Anish they were going to pick up Diya but found him sleeping on a bench near the reception. She knew it was quite stressful for Anish as well and decided not to wake him. She left Anish sleeping there and joined Adi in the car. They drove away from the hospital while Anish remained peacefully asleep, unaware of the situation. The car headed towards Diya's apartment. A silent understanding was passing between Adi and Tanya as they navigated through the empty streets.

They drove through the quiet streets of the ITPL area. Tanya suddenly asked, "Do you think Joy could try to commit suicide?" The question surprised Adi, leaving him unsettled. The word "suicide" echoed in his mind and started troubling him.

Seeing Adi's discomfort, Tanya immediately tried to change the subject.

Adi, surprised by the question, responded quickly: "No, no, that's not it. He was stressed, just drinking to relax, and probably fell down accidentally."

Despite his explanation, Adi couldn't shake the idea of "suicide." It continued to trouble him, making him feel uneasy. The car moved quietly through the streets, the gravity of the situation weighing heavily on both of them as they thought about Joy's condition.

Adi's mind raced like a wild horse, with thousands of thoughts flowing around, both good and bad, distracting his focus. In this turmoil, he found a little relief in memories from their days in the PG, transporting him back to the past. The memory of the time when Joy proposed to Diya.

Diya was Joy's classmate in engineering. She was studying for her MBA in Bangalore at the time. Joy and Diya shared a special bond from their days in college. Adi had played a role in bringing them closer, which briefly eased his mind. However, the troubling thought of "suicide" still lingered.

Lost in memories, Adi recalled the day when he and Joy went to Marathahalli for shopping. Marathahalli was a lively area with plenty of options near their PG. In the middle of the busy market, Joy was deeply occupied with the phone.

Adi got a chance to tease him. He poked Joy, "Talking to Diya, hmm?"

Joy, with a nod, confirmed, "Yes."

Unable to resist, Adi poked again, "Have you proposed to her?"

Joy, visibly nervous, admitted, "No... not yet."

Adi tried to encourage his friend; he urged, "Come on, buddy. You've got to take the leap before someone else beats you to it. She is a nice girl. You'll regret it if you don't propose to her."

Joy, his apparent apprehension, confessed, "I just can't gather the courage. Whenever I try, I freeze."

Adi, trying to act like a love guru, reassured, "You're a grown man, Joy. Do not get afraid about the result. Remember, Mard ko dard nahi hota hai (man does not feel pain). Just go for it."

Joy retorted, with a hint of sarcasm, "Oh, sure, it's easy for you to say. But if she says no? Then I'll lose her as a friend too. You know what? Even men feel pain, too. Sala Mard ko bhi dard hota hai! And sometimes, it hurts even more when it hits odd places. Don't get me wrong, I'm referring to the heart here!"

Both burst out laughing.

They finished shopping and started walking through the bustling market to the parking area.

Adi then said, "Joy, what if I propose to her?"

Joy replied in shock, "Dude, I thought you were my friend. Now you want to propose to my girl?"

Adi's expression was even more surprising: "Hey, calm down, Joy! I meant, what if I propose to her on your behalf, not for myself, buddy? Ahh… But if she turns you down, maybe I can try my luck. Who knows? She might say yes to me. I am single, too."

Joy laughed and said, "You're such a rascal, man."

After a few moments of silence, Joy added, "No, let's not do that now. I'll propose to her when the time is right."

The two friends shared a hearty laugh, then hopped on the bike to ride back to the PG with a bottle of Old Monk in hand.

As they reached their nest in the Happy PG, Adi poured 2 pegs of drink, setting the mood with the familiar beats of "Maiya Maiya," one of his favourite songs. Joy couldn't help but ask, "What's with this song? You listen to it all the time."

Adi smiled and replied, "It's not about the song; I just love the movie. And the song reminds me about it."

Joy nodded in recognition. "Guru, right?"

"Yes," confirmed Adi. "The movie was inspired by the journey of Dhirubhai Ambani," he added. Adi then paused and took a deep breath, then continued again, "One day, I'll build my empire too…. Like him."

Joy smiled. "You started again? Always talking about building an empire. But what's the point of having a lot of money? Is money everything?"

Adi's expression turned serious as he responded, "Money may not be everything, but it certainly gives you the power to influence things in your favour."

Joy calmly took a sip of his drink, expressing doubt about the transformative power of wealth.

As they enjoyed the warmth of Old Monk, they got caught up in a conversation about dreams, money, and chasing success.

Adi took a comfortable seat in the corner of his bed. Leaning back on the pillow, he continued, "You see, it's a narrative that's spread among ordinary people to discourage them from dreaming big and to keep them grounded. We romanticise poverty—do you know why?"

He went on to answer his own question: "It's because the rich have programmed us that way. Wealth is like energy; neither can be created nor destroyed; it's always moving from person to person. So, if the poor start thinking about wealth, the rich have to share the pie."

Intrigued, Joy listened closely as Adi continued to explain.

He kept going with enthusiasm. "Let me give you an example. Imagine Ram and Shyam both selling apples in the same market. If Ram's sales increase, Shyam's will decrease. If everyone aspired to be rich, the wealth of the rich would decline. So, it's essential to have ordinary people, or 'Praja' (common people) as they say, for a king to govern. Otherwise, who would they rule over?"

With every sip of the rum, the discussion intensified, fuelled by the powerful kick of the Old Monk.

Joy: "So, you want to be a king?"

Adi replied strongly, "Definitely. You know, a king isn't different from us; they aren't specially-abled. A king has only one thing special: the ability to take risks, to be at the forefront, and to own his or her actions. Others are afraid to do so; they always need someone in the front as a leader, a guru, or a legend. That's the reason why millions are ruled by a single person. People love to follow; they love to be ruled."

Joy tried to ease the conversation, saying, "This is something that always goes over my head. I'm just a simple middle-class boy, having a job like my father, wanting to enjoy life."

But Adi's frustration boiled over after listening to Joy's middle-class thoughts, his voice now carrying an edge of anger.

"That's the wrong attitude! Are you enjoying today? Living in a shared room in a PG, checking price tags three times before buying anything. An entire life of compromise!"

Joy remained calm, replying with a glimpse of a smile, "Relax, buddy. Don't think too much. What can we do?"

Adi's voice turned passionate. "We can try! Try to learn, set up something, and be big and powerful!"

Joy had no choice but to accept the defeat, knowing that arguments after drinks lead nowhere. He agreed, "Okay, sorry, sir. My mistake. We will be powerful tomorrow. Now, let's play some music and pour another peg."

As they were about to dive into another round, Joy's phone buzzed with a text message from Diya. The incoming message caught Adi's attention, prompting him to swiftly snatch Joy's phone.

Joy (surprised): "What are you doing?"

Adi replied calmly, "Don't worry. I'll show it to you before sending anything. Or you'll be stuck forever in the friend zone."

The liquid courage from the rum had seemingly infused Joy with a newfound confidence. He agreed to Adi with a smirk.

Adi proceeded to open Diya's message, which was a simple "Good night."

Adi's Response: "Okay..."

Joy's face was twisted in disbelief. "Who responds with 'okay' to a good night message?" he wondered. And with no time, I realised the decision to hand over the phone to Adi was a big mistake. As this guy does not know how to talk to girls, he is far better than him in this area.

Diya replied. "Okay, good night."

Adi, maintaining his mysterious behaviour, deliberately delayed his response and eventually typed, "Hmm."

Joy, now thoroughly puzzled, questioned Adi's act of drama with monosyllabic replies.

Adi tried to explain to him, "I believe she likes you. If that's the case, she'll be curious why you're behaving oddly all of a sudden."

Joy: "But she said good night, and you replied with 'Hmm.' What now?"

Adi: (confidently) "Just wait; she'll text again." The anticipation lingered as they awaited Diya's next move in this interesting exchange.

Diya's reply arrived promptly, and with Adi's urging, Joy handed over the phone with a smile. He now realised the mind game Adi was trying to play.

Diya replied, "Are you upset? Is there something bothering you?"

Adi, playing Joy's role, responded with a mischievous tone:

Adi: "Yes."

Diya: "What?"

Adi: "I don't know."

Diya: "What happened to you? Please tell me. Did I do anything wrong?"

Adi, continuing the playful act

"What do you think about me?"

Diya: "What type of question is this? You are a nice guy. You are my good friend."

Adi, pushing the envelope and steering directly into unfamiliar territory, dropped the bomb:

"That's the problem. I don't want to be friend-zoned."

The room fell into an anticipatory silence as they awaited Diya's reaction. Her reply was noticeably absent, and the atmosphere tensed. Joy's face turned red with the pressure of the situation, and he took a gulp from his peg, bottomed up, and started walking around the room.

Joy: "I told you not to poke. Now she won't talk to me anymore."

Adi, maintaining his calm demeanour, responded sagely:

"This is what I was talking about. If you want to win, you have to take risks. Tell me one thing: has anyone ever won who has never played? You have to step out and hit; leave the rest to luck."

Joy just ignored it with a "Hmm." Odd silence filled the room, and then suddenly, the phone buzzed again.

Diya: "Shall I call?"

Adi, maintaining the facade, replied coolly, "It's okay; no need to give me sympathy," and handed the phone back to Joy.

The phone rang… Joy answered the call… The tension in the room escalated.

Joy: "Yes, Diya."

Diya: "You're a friend, so you're in that zone. Have you ever shared your feelings, idiot? What are you drinking tonight that has given you this much courage?"

Joy, with a scared voice, tried to make up for the situation: "Sorry, Diya, I... didn't want to hurt you."

Diya: "Shut up. Say what you need to say."

Joy did not know what to say. Complete silence for a few moments from both ends. Diya then said, "What, Mr. Ganguly? You were saying something. Is all courage finished?"

Joy was struggling to say that he loved her more than anything in the world, but the words were not ready to come out of his mouth.

After a lot of struggles with his inner self, he started fumbling nervously: "I... I... I love you."

Adi continued to drive, while the sweet old memories played in his mind, giving him some sense of peace inside. Unconsciously, he pressed the sudden brake—there was a police patrol ahead. They were conducting drunk-driving checks near Silk Board Signal, and Adi lost in his thoughts, hadn't realised that he was about to hit the barricade.

The policeman knocked on the window, and Adi lowered it. He requested that Adi blow into the alcohol checker. Adi complied, and the result was obviously below the limit. Adi had no alcohol that night. The policeman tapped the vehicle as a sign to move, and Adi started driving again.

The incident disrupted the continuous stream of thoughts that occupied his mind.

Diya's residence was in the BTM 2nd stage, a short distance from the signal. Adi crossed Silk Board Signal, took a right turn at the petrol pump, and, in the next left turn, they stopped.

Tanya picked up her phone and dialled Diya's number. "We're outside of your apartment," she said as Diya answered.

In 5 minutes, a tall girl emerged from the apartment across the road. That's Diya. She was quite tall, taller than the average girls wearing a regular jeans top, her long hair fluttering in the breeze. She had no makeup on but wore innocence on her face. This innocence was the signature of Diya, who always reminded Adi of how perfect she was for his best friend. Both of them were such simple and easy-going individuals, unlike Adi, who tended to complicate things and create problems for others.

Chapter 4

TALE OF FRIENDSHIP

The hospital corridors were tense, and the team of doctors guided Joy, lying on the stretcher bed, towards the brightly lit entrance of the operation theatre. Adi, Diya, and Tanya stood together, supporting each other. Their faces filled with worry, and their eyes locked on Joy's fading presence, each heartbeat echoing with hope and fear. Each step of the way seemed to elongate, the echoes of their footfalls bouncing off the walls, amplifying the gravity of the situation.

As they waited in the lobby, their minds surged with a mixture of hope and fear. Adi tried to stay calm but looked worried. Diya, usually happy, was solemn, holding Tanya's hand. Tanya, the youngest in the group, bit her lip nervously, thinking about what might be happening to Joy on the other side of the doors.

Meanwhile, Anish, unaware of what was happening, lay stretched across the uncomfortable hospital benches. He was lost in a deep sleep, his mouth hanging open, emitting a chorus of loud snores that broke the tense silence.

Suddenly, they heard someone calling out, "Adi..."

Shocked, Adi turned to see a towering figure—a six-foot-six middle-aged man, neatly trimmed, with a kind smile, Shukla bhaiya. Relief washed over Adi as he spotted Shukla bhaiya after such a long time. They hadn't seen each other since they left the PG. Adi warmly hugged Shukla, grateful for his familiar presence in this moment of uncertainty.

Shukla explained that Anish had informed him the last night and inquired about Joy's condition. Adi, glad for the chance to take his mind off things, told Shukla about the scary accident and what the doctors said about Joy's condition.

As they were talking, Adi realised he hadn't introduced Diya and Tanya yet and quickly fixed the mistake, ensuring that Shukla bhaiya was familiar with everyone present there.

Adi, pointing to Diya, "Shukla bhaiya, she is Diya, Joy's girlfriend."

Diya: "Hello, Bhaiya."

Adi continued, "And she is Tanya."

Shukla bhaiya, looking curious, asked, "Your girlfriend?"

Tanya refused with a shy smile. "No, just a friend."

Shukla bhaiya, with a playful smile, said, "Got it. Where is Anish?"

They turned to see Anish still fast asleep on the hospital bench.

Shukla bhaiya smiled. "This motu hasn't changed a bit. So, what's next? There's no point in nervously waiting here. How about we grab some tea at the canteen?"

They hesitated at first but eventually agreed.

Walking to the hospital canteen, Shukla brought up a memory from the past to lighten the heavy atmosphere. He could see the worry in their eyes.

Shukla began, "Adi, remember that night when Anish disappeared, and we searched everywhere for him?"

Adi replied, "How can we forget that night?"

Shukla turned to the girls and asked, "Do you girls know the story?"

They both shook their heads.

"Okay, let me tell you the story," said Shukla.

Adi was about to interrupt Shukla, thinking it might not be the right time, but then realised Shukla bhaiya's intention and said, "Sure, but let's order the tea first."

They ordered 4 cups of tea and settled at a table near the window. The hustle and bustle of the traffic heading towards Whitefield can be clearly observed here. With the first sip of the tea, Shukla bhaiya took it upon himself to lighten the dull mood with tales of Anish.

Despite trying, an unspoken fear hung over all of them. Diya couldn't stop thinking about the events of last night. She wondered if breaking up with Joy caused his current situation. Questions raced through her mind, overshadowing the warmth of the tea in her hand.

Shukla smiled and turned to Diya and Tanya. He started telling the story of their past. "You might know this," he began, "we all lived in a PG called 'Happy PG' in

Mahadevapura back then. It was the beginning of a career for most of us."

Shukla patiently continued, "Well, in those days, our celebrations mainly revolved around the Old Monk. Every small victory or setback was marked with a drink. But with limited funds, we tried to drink in moderation, convincing ourselves it wasn't good for our health."

He continued, "But after one bottle…"

Diya chimed in, her voice tinged with a hint of sadness, "Yes, after one bottle, all the madness comes out. Without thinking about others' emotions. The pain we are feeling now, waiting for news from the operation theatre."

Shukla understood Diya's concern; he kept things casual and continued, "So, that day, Anish and Adi went to get some drinks. Anish stayed outside with a cigarette, while Adi went inside the bar to buy them. Now, here's what happened: a police raid suddenly happened, and the bartender…"

Tanya interrupted, asking why.

Adi explained: "It was almost 1 a.m., and the shop shouldn't have been open that late, according to the rules."

Tanya nodded, getting it. "Okay, keep going."

Adi signalled to Shukla to continue.

Shukla continued, "When the police arrived, the bartenders quickly turned off the lights and closed the shutters. Meanwhile, Adi was stuck inside with a couple of other customers."

Tanya was very curious; she asked again, "And what about Anish?"

Shukla bhaiya grinned. "That's where the real story begins. The police knocked on the shutters, and there was probably some deal between the bar owners and the police. Eventually, they left. Adi came out with a bottle of Old Monk, but the problem was that Anish wasn't there outside."

Adi thought Anish might have gone back to the PG after seeing the police, so he went back to where Kesarilal and I were waiting. But as Adi returned to the room and told us what happened. We all got worried about where Anish might be. And finally, despite being drunk, the three of us had to rush out with 2 bikes."

"The wine shop was on the Whitefield main road, so our first instinct was to check that side, thinking Anish might be somewhere around there. We were really worried at that time—kind of scared, you could say—that we forgot to consider the dangers of riding bikes while drunk and without helmets. All we cared about was finding Anish, no matter what."

"After about half an hour of panicked searching, we stopped opposite Phoenix Mall, debating whether the police had arrested Anish and if it was necessary for us to head to the police station. We were worried about who would be brave enough to talk to the police. We were all nervous about dealing with them, especially since we were drunk. Plus, we didn't know why the police might have captured Anish."

"While discussing, we thought having some tea might help us think more clearly. So, we bought 3 cups of tea and some cigarettes from a late-night tea vendor. And guess what? As we walked away from the main street to the side lane while smoking, we found something surprising."

Diya stayed quiet; her attention fully captured by the unfolding story. Adi's face brightened with a smile, and Tanya, overcome with curiosity, eagerly asked, "What happened next?"

With a playful smile, Shukla kept telling his story: "There used to be an optical store; maybe it's still there, with a narrow passage beside it. We found Anish there, asleep, hugging a street dog."

Diya couldn't help but break into a smile at the heartwarming image, while Tanya, feeling a mix of concern and laughter, questioned, "Was he okay?"

Adi couldn't control himself and interrupted, "So, when I was stuck inside the shop, he started walking towards Phoenix Mall in fear of the police. Once there, he bought tea and biscuits and decided to feed the dogs while having a cup of tea. But being high, he eventually fell asleep there."

Tanya exclaimed, "Oh my God, Anish is so adorable!"

All of a sudden, they heard Anish from behind, his voice sounding sleepy, asking, "What's happening? Why didn't you guys wake me up?"

They all burst into laughter at the unexpected interruption.

The tea was all gone, and they thought to head back towards the operation theatre. It had been more than an hour since the operation began.

❖ ❖ ❖

The tension grew stronger again, overcoming the lightness of Shukla's story, as they got closer to the gate of the operation theatre.

Out of nowhere, Shukla asked, "Adi, did you inform Joy's father?"

Adi replied, "Yes, Bhaiya. Anish already did that."

Anish added, "I got a message from uncle. He caught an early morning flight and landed in Bangalore."

Feeling a bit unsure, Diya asked, "Should I stay here when his father arrives?"

Adi comforted her, "Don't worry, Diya. I'm sure uncle knows about you."

All of a sudden, the door of the operation theatre opened, and Dr Chaitanya came out. He smiled at Anish and Adi before sharing the news: "He's okay now. Thank goodness the injury wasn't too bad. But there's something you all need to know we found sleeping pills in his blood. We need to talk about it."

The doctor hurried to his office, and Adi and Shukla walked with him.

The doctor nodded, "There were too many pills in his body. If there were any more, he might have died from them. I think we should treat this as a suicide attempt."

Adi expressed his worries: "Doctor, I hope you recognise me and your patient."

The doctor confirmed, "Yes, I've seen you both in the news."

Adi pleaded, "These are just allegations. We're regular businessmen. He might have tried to calm himself with the pills for a good sleep."

The doctor did not answer anything and went into his office.

Adi felt lost outside the doctor's office. He shared his concern with Shukla, "Bhaiya, this suicide story could make things worse for us."

Shukla calmly suggested, "You go back and be with Diya and Taniya; I'll speak with the doctor. Maybe he took extra pills while drunk. It need not be intentional."

Adi shook his head and walked back to the operation theatre gate. Meanwhile, Diya was devastated after hearing about the sleeping pills. Tears were rolling down from her eyes, making their way through her cheeks. She felt overwhelmed with guilt feelings, blaming herself for the situation. When Adi returned, Diya's emotions erupted, unleashing a flood of accusations aimed at him. She believed Adi was responsible for what happened, stating that his constant pursuit of success had led Joy into this dangerous situation.

Trying to calm the situation, Anish stepped in and said, "Please, Diya …," but she was taken by the emotions and not ready to listen to anyone.

Tanya could not take the blame on Adi; she managed to break through the tension, her voice calm yet firm, "Diya, I understand your fear and the pain you're experiencing; I can't even share it with you. But why blame Adi? Look at his face; can't you see the pain he's going through? And as for the business, everyone is pointing fingers. If we, as friends and family, don't support them, what kind of relationship do we have? Remember, they're accused, not proven guilty. We need to stand by our loved ones through thick and thin."

Adi, touched by Tanya's strong support, felt a newfound connection with her. Perhaps it was the sincerity in her words or the empathy in her eyes as she stood up for him.

Interrupting the growing tension, Adi intervened,

"It's okay, everyone. We're all under immense pressure, all feeling frustrated. Let's not argue amongst ourselves. Diya, I'm really sorry for anything and everything I did that might have made things worse. Let me fix this. I promise I'll do everything I can to make it right."

Meanwhile, the nurses wheeled Joy to his room, he was now in a stable condition. One of them noticed Diya's distress, offering a comforting smile, she assured her, "He is resting comfortably, just asleep from the anaesthesia. You can visit him in 3 hours."

With the departure of the medical staff, Shukla approached Adi, his voice lowered to a whisper, "Don't worry, Adi. The doctor understood the situation."

Adi breathed a sigh of relief, expressing his gratitude, "Thank you, Bhaiya."

Anish's phone started ringing – it was Joy's father.

Anish answered, "Yes, uncle."

On the other end, Joy's father asked anxiously, "I'm at the hospital reception. Where should I come?"

Quickly taking the phone from Anish, Adi responded, "uncle, please wait there; we're coming in 2 minutes."

Hurrying to the reception area, they spotted an old man waiting with a mix of worry and hope written all over his face. His grey hair framed his worried face, and his eyes showed deep concern. He looked like a powerless parent, waiting anxiously for news about his son.

At that moment, all the other issues - the business troubles, the legal fight, even the questions of who was right or wrong - seemed to fade away. For this father, his only concern was his son lying in the hospital bed, fighting for his life. It's a feeling that's hard to put into words, the worry and fear a parent feels when their child is in trouble. It's like everything else just doesn't matter anymore; all that matters is the health and well-being of their loved ones. That's the kind of suffering this father was experiencing as he waited at the reception just to know that his son was all well.

Adi reached to him and touched his feet. It's A gesture of respect deeply rooted in our Indian culture, where we believe God lives in everyone. The old man grasped Adi's shoulder, his voice loaded with concern, "How is he now?"

Adi tried to reduce his fears; he assured him, "Uncle, please don't worry. Joy suffered a fall, injuring the back of his head. The doctor performed a minor surgery, and he's currently resting in his cabin. They'll inform us once he wakes up."

The father understood the situation but was not able to wait. He was eager to see his son, and asked, "Can I see him?"

Anish was quick to respond, "Yes, uncle. Come with me; you can see him from outside the room."

The old man, accompanied by Anish, rushed towards Joy's cabin. He was hopeful yet anxious about what he might find there.

Meanwhile, Shukla leaned in close to Adi, his voice hushed, "Let's keep the sleeping pills incident away from uncle for now." Adi too nodded in agreement, acknowledging the wisdom in Shukla bhaiya's suggestion.

After some time, Anish returned alone. It seemed that Joy's father preferred to wait outside the cabin.

Taking charge, Adi asked everyone, "Why don't you all head to the waiting area? I'll bring uncle out here." With that, Adi made his way towards Joy's cabin.

Chapter 5

HARMONY IN HARDSHIP

Joy's father looked really worried, walking back and forth in the corridor, unable to hide how anxious he felt. Losing his wife not long ago made Joy even more important to him. Now, seeing his son in trouble, it was tough for him to stay strong in front of everyone.

Shukla felt the tension mounting as they waited for Joy to wake up. He suggested Adi ask the nurse about Joy's condition since it had been 3 hours since he was moved to the room. But before Adi could do anything, Joy's father asked them to be patient and trust the doctors to keep them updated.

In between, Anish brought pastries and snacks, hoping to bring some comfort. "Uncle, have some food. You must be hungry," he said, offering the tray of snacks to Joy's father.

Joy's father politely refused; he was too worried to eat. "I'm not hungry, beta (Son). You all eat," he replied, his attention still on the closed doors of Joy's cabin.

Despite the tense atmosphere, Shukla stepped up, encouraging everyone to have a pastry. "Anish brought these for us. Let's eat a little," he urged, his voice calm and comforting. "Joy will get better, and we'll see him soon. But we need to take care of ourselves too," He tried to convince everyone to have some food, as none of them had anything since morning.

Shukla bhaiya's words made sense to all. The group agreed, and each took a pastry. In Shukla bhaiya's presence, they found strength and reassurance. Adi and Anish remembered Sukhla Bhaiya's role as a leader during their PG days.

Four hours passed since the operation ended, and the clock now showed 2 pm. The bustling morning activities in the hospital had settled down as staff members took a well-deserved break after their lunch, creating a momentary calm in the usual flurry of activity.

Hospitals are interesting places with many different emotions mixed together. In one corner sat a young couple, likely waiting for a pregnancy check-up. They seemed happy about becoming parents but also a bit nervous, which is normal for expectant parents. An old man in the center was waiting in a wheelchair, for the nurse to come and wheel him. His eyes conveyed weariness, reflecting his acceptance that his time in this world was drawing to a close. On the other side, a young man was alone, looking troubled, as if he were dealing with difficult thoughts."

Around 2:30 pm, a nurse came from the ward, her smile carrying a glimmer of hope as she delivered promising news. "Your patient is awake now. We've served him lunch. You may go in to see him, but please remember, only 2 visitors at a time," she said.

The group exchanged relieved looks, feeling eager as they got ready to enter Joy's room. Tanya kindly said, "Uncle, why don't you go in first? We'll come right after you."

Joy's father accepted the offer without hesitation. Shukla added, "She asked if 2 could go, so Diya, why don't you join uncle?" Diya, feeling a bit unprepared, agreed with hesitation. She wasn't entirely sure how much Joy's father knew about their relationship, but it was evident why Shukla bhaiya suggested she accompany him.

Joy's father entered the cabin, and Diya followed.

Joy was sitting up in bed, wearing a blue hospital gown. Tubes and channels were still attached to his left side, a reminder of the medical procedures he had undergone. His head was wrapped in a white bandage.

Upon seeing his father, Joy tried to avoid eye contact, a sense of shame evident in his expression. However, his father asked, with a warm smile, "How are you feeling, beta?"

Joy, with a hint of tears in his eyes, replied, "Sorry, baba."

His father reassured him, "Don't be sorry. I understand the pressure you are going through."

Joy, still emotional, admitted, "I made you ashamed, baba."

His father responded, "Not at all, my son. You've dared to dream big, something which I never did in my life. Not many from our middle-class background would have dared. Only those with courage can dream big and alter their destiny. I am proud of you."

Joy, with tearful eyes, expressed his concerns, "But baba, these people, the court, the media..."

His father smiled and said, "There's a famous saying, my child. If people start talking about you, understand that you've done something beyond their imagination."

Continuing with words of wisdom, he said, "There will be a hundred hurdles when you try to move a stone, but don't be like me and step back. Never stop trying. I hope everything will be sorted out soon. I know you cannot cheat anyone, can you?"

Joy, with sincerity in his eyes, replied, "No, baba."

Diya stood at a distance, quietly observing as Joy's father called her closer. "Why are you standing there? Come closer. I never thought I would meet you in the hospital. Joy told me about you. I am very happy to see you, beta," he said warmly.

Diya felt speechless, the situation leaving her feeling numb. She felt shy hearing Joy's father's kind words. She stole a glance at Joy, feeling something stirring inside her. It wasn't bad; it was a feeling of happiness. Seeing Joy safe erased all her worries. Her complaints to Joy vanished from her mind as if Joy's father's wise words washed them away. Suddenly, she felt strong. She wanted to be with Joy, holding his hand through this storm, no matter what happened.

Diya hadn't seen her father since she was small. Seeing Joy's father encourage him made her see a father figure in him.

With a bright smile and relief in his eyes, Joy's father came out of the cabin. Adi walked up to him, smiling, and asked, "How is he, uncle?"

Joy's father replied, "He's fine. Go and talk to your friend. He needs you."

Adi nodded and hurried into the cabin. Tanya glanced at Shukla bhaiya, who smiled and said, "Go; Anish and I will meet him after you."

Adi entered with Taniya, and a mix of emotions overwhelmed him. On the one hand, he was happy to see Joy safe, while on the other, a sense of guilt lingered in his mind, holding himself responsible for the situation. Taniya greeted Joy, "Hello, Joy. So, how are you?"

Joy, with a smile, replied, "Not so good, Yaar."

Adi, overcome with emotion, apologised, "Sorry, Yaar. You are going through a lot for me."

Joy reassured him with a big smile, "No, Adi. We started this together. Maybe the idea was yours, but I have done my best to make it a success."

Adi, tears welling up, "Agreed; so true."

Tanya intervened, "Guys, now stop being a child. You both can't break down like this. You have to fight back, get well soon, and get ready for the second part of the fight. I am sure you both will prove everyone wrong, just like you did before."

Joy echoed the sentiment, "Yes, like we did before."

Adi, wiping his tears, said, "Yes, Joy. We can do it again. Do not worry. I will fix everything."

Joy, a touch of sarcasm in his voice, remarked, "Yes, true. You always have a plan."

Adi smiled, "Well, Anish and Shukla bhaiya are waiting outside. I'll send them in. They've been waiting to meet you for a long time."

Joy nodded in surprise. "Shukla bhaiya?"

Adi opened the door and nodded to signal Shukla bhaiya and Anish to go inside and meet Joy.

Outside the cabin, Adi observed the atmosphere lighten up with laughter. Shukla bhaiya, Anish, Diya, and uncle shared a funny moment, laughing together. The heavy atmosphere of tension began to disappear.

Joy's face lit up with excitement when he saw Shukla bhaiya. "How are you, Bhaiya? It's been so long!" he exclaimed.

Shukla playfully replied, "Ah, yes, just your average working-class guy here. Unlike you, Mr. Entrepreneur. When do you ever find time to catch up with us?"

Joy, feeling a bit ashamed, responded, "No, Bhaiya, it's not like that. You know how things have been lately."

Shukla assured him, "Do not worry. I was just pulling your leg. I was always in touch with Anish, and he used to share all the updates about you and Adi."

Anish was about to say something when Joy interrupted, "He's always like a news channel, but this time he did well. At least we met after such a long time."

Anish smiled, claiming, "I always do well only."

Joy looked at Shukla bhaiya, and both burst into laughter. After a minute of shared laughter, Shukla began,

"Yes, Joy, he does everything right."

Shukla looked at Anish with an adorable glance and said, "Yaar, I am happy to have a friend like you. You always do right. I could write a complete book on you."

Joy smiled and said, "But thank you, Anish, for bringing me here on time."

Anish modestly responded, "Nothing to thank for. For you, I had to sleep on the hospital bench last night."

Shukla started, teasing Anish again, "But it's better than the footpath, right? Anyways, Anish is an expert at sleeping on the footpath or finding public properties, especially at night, right Joy?"

Joy smiled and said, "You still remember?"

Shukla, with a touch of emotion in his voice, replied, "How can I forget, Joy? Those days were the foundation of our lives. Maybe the pocket wasn't full, but life was full of fun and love. I still remember those days. Whenever I am alone, I smile to myself and miss you guys badly. I share those stories on almost every occasion. Everyone in my circle now knows all of you, though they've never met you."

Anish innocently chimed in, "That's okay, but what did I find at night?"

Joy teased him, "Try to remember what you bought when we were in Coorg."

Anish thought for some time and then continued with a big smile "Oh, that's because of you only. You asked me."

"Joy tried to deny it, saying, 'Shukla bhaiya, that's not true. Anish was excited that night, remember? We were at the campfire, and Anish suggested,

"I can go to the market and bring more chicken if required."

"I told him that we were in a remote homestay, and there was nothing nearby except tea gardens. But he insisted, saying he saw a shop there. Everyone advised against it."

Anish admitted adorably, "Oh yeah, that was a mistake."

Shukla bhaiya reminisced, "And you remember even the homestay guys locked their doors and slept. It was almost midnight, I guess."

Joy confirmed, "Yes, approximately. And the bad part is he (pointing to Anish) dragged me with him, and I became part of the story."

Anish interrupted, "But trust me, taking the bench was Joy's idea, not mine."

Shukla couldn't help but laugh; he added, "I still remember when we saw you two coming back with the broken bus stop bench on your shoulders. Adi was rolling on the ground with laughter."

Joy chimed in, "When we went out, he (pointing to Anish) made me walk so long, saying he knows a shop here that stays open late. But we were only walking on an empty street and then reached a little wider road where there was a bus stop. We decided to rest on the bus stop bench. Then I asked him to go back, but he was like, 'No, we can't go back empty-handed.' After a lot of research and discussion, we decided to take the bench."

All of them laughed again.

Shukla bhaiya teased, "But how did you pull it out? Wasn't it locked to the floor?"

Anish explained, "Yes, it was, but it was a bit loose. We both pulled, and it came out."

Shukla and Anish exchanged a look, finding peace in seeing Joy laughing. They told Joy to rest and not to worry, then stepped out of the cabin.

Chapter 6

THE IDEA

Adi, Taniya, and Diya finished their lunch; though it was pretty late, they really needed this meal after spending the entire night at the hospital.

Shukla bhaiya left for his office after the meeting with Joy. Joy's father accompanied Anish to Joy's apartment, while Diya joined Adi and Tanya at Adi's place.

The evening visiting hours will start again at 7 pm and go on until 8.30 pm. So, they tried to rest for a while before heading back to the hospital in the evening. But Adi broke the silence all of a sudden, his expression filled with uncertainty.

"I want both of you to know something, especially you, Diya. Since you and Joy are in a relationship, this could affect your future. It's great that both you and Tanya have faith in us and are standing by us during these troubled days. But I think it's crucial for you to know how it all started. Then you can decide where you stand."

A sudden shadow covered both Diya and Tanya.

Diya responded, 'What do you mean? Have you guys really done something wrong?'

Adi clarified, 'No, Diya.'

Diya insisted, 'Then I don't need to know anything.'

Before Diya could continue, Adi interrupted, 'But not entirely right either.'

The atmosphere of the room filled with a sense of suspense.

Tanya questioned, "Adi, what do you mean?"

Adi explained, "To understand everything, you need to know the entire story—how we started and what we did right or wrong."

Diya, impatient, said, "Okay, we are listening."

Adi continued, "This all began about 6 years back when Joy and I were sharing a PG. That's where we met, and, as you've heard bits of our story, we quickly became good friends. Along with Anish, Shukla bhaiya, Kesarilal, and others, we formed a tight-knit group. We spent most of our free time together, throwing parties, engaging in deep discussions, and having daily debates that became a routine part of our lives."

As Adi talked about the past, it was clear that their friendship was more than just shared living space and casual banter. It was a safe space where they supported each other's dreams, even though they didn't have much money. The PG was like a centre for sharing thoughts and ideas.

Adi went on, "During those days, like many middle-class individuals, we also had big dreams but faced the harsh reality of limited financial resources. Our discussions frequently centred around topics such as money, career advancement, business concepts, skill development, and the desire for a better life."

Joy was different from the others; his dream was to be a painter and share his art in exhibitions. Meanwhile, I was always on the lookout for opportunities to launch new businesses by addressing real-life problems."

Adi continued, explaining, "It's been said that when you desire something with all of your heart, the universe helps to make it happen. You become so consumed by your dreams that you start noticing things you've never paid attention to before."

Something similar happened to me one day when I was riding back to the PG from work. I saw a dreadful accident where a young biker collided with an elderly man. Both were severely injured. The crowd gathered, but despite the gathering, few stepped forward to help. Some even started filming the scene without helping the victims. A few kind-hearted folks offered some water. I felt terribly helpless, not knowing the local hospital. I was completely clueless about how to help.

In the middle of the chaos, suggestions ranged from calling emergency helplines to involving the police. Some suggested reporting the incident at the next traffic signal. A few tried to arrange transportation to the hospital, but no passing cars stopped to assist. The victims continued to bleed, and after some time, two traffic police officers arrived on a bike. They struggled to find an auto-rickshaw to take the injured to the nearest hospital.

That incident deeply upset me. During the rest of my ride home, I couldn't shake off the thoughts of whether they would survive. Witnessing the lack of efficient emergency infrastructure, I found my problem statement. Excitement rushed within me, and numerous solutions started flooding my mind. I ran to my room, opened my laptop, and, unaware of the formal business plan, started drafting my ideas in a PowerPoint presentation. It covered the problem statement, solutions, market size, competitions, limitations, and how we could monetise the concept and so on."

Tanya interrupted, "But Adi, you run an IT consulting company that provides services to product-based companies. Your business is nowhere related to medical or emergency services."

Adi smiled, saying, "The entire story is hidden in the details. Sometimes, it's not something you see."

Diya expressed her confusion, "I am confused now. I can't relate to your story. I knew Joy before you both started the business. I remember Joy saying that you were working on some prototypes and facing challenges like the need for a technical team and finance. But then he mentioned that the idea changed, and now you have finance to set up a consulting company."

Adi nodded, "You heard it correctly. I'll tell you everything. I don't want to hide anything from you guys anymore."

Tanya urged, "Okay, please continue. Let us know what else you guys have hidden from us till now."

Adi continued, his eyes reflecting a mix of determination and vulnerability,

"So, I found a solution – community-driven medical emergency support, along with an SOS service for critical situations like accidents and assistance for the elderly staying alone.

I drafted all my ideas on PowerPoint slides, and when Joy returned from the office. I shared the idea with him. You know how Joy's nature is, always eager to help; he delved into a deeper discussion on the pros and cons of the services and the various others we could implement.

I can very well recall how excited we were that we spent the entire night discussing different aspects of the idea.

The next day, after work, I brought up the topic with Joy again. However, this time, his response wasn't the same. He told me, 'It's good to dream, but it's beyond our capacity. Who will build the tech? Where will we get the finances? After all this, none of us knows anything about starting a business.'

His concerns were absolutely correct, but I was not ready to give up. I began learning about startups, registering a company, corporate laws, how to raise funding, etc. Meanwhile, my quest continued to find like-minded people who could code to build the prototype.

This was all ongoing when suddenly, Shukla bhaiya got a hefty package and shifted to Koramangala. On the other hand, Kesarilal couldn't find a job, so he had to work as a waiter in a nearby restaurant. Anish managed to get a job offer, but just before he was supposed to start, the company told him that they had to put the position on hold, leaving him unsure about what would happen next.

The changes affected everyone in the PG. Kesarilal and Anish started staying silent, always tense, avoiding social gatherings. Joy and I understood that the reason was nothing but financial difficulties. We tried to help them wherever possible.

However, the situation got worse, as Kesarilal had to quit the journey because his father was on his deathbed and needed him to support the family. With a heavy heart, we had to say goodbye to him. He went back to his village and, as far as I know, started farming.

Our group broke apart; Joy, Anish, and I were the ones left behind, feeling the sadness that grasped over our lively PG. Our once Happy PG turned into an unhappy place for us."

Adi's story continues, "As time passed, I gained a good understanding of forming a company and investment options, and I made some contacts. I also managed to convince two more guys from the IT department of my office to work with me on this. Now, I needed to convince Joy to join. I knew he was the best person to partner with – honest, tremendously dedicated, and a talented artist. Having him on board meant we could also manage app design and other marketing-related artworks in-house, along with his tech expertise. However, Joy was not ready to step out of his middle-class 9-to-5 mindset.

But the story took a turn that day when Joy came home early; he was visibly disturbed and angry. He threw his bag on the bed and went out. I was confused, started searching for him, and finally found him alone on the terrace, smoking. I went near him and asked him what was wrong. I saw tears in his eyes; he was broken completely and replied, 'I was expecting a promotion.'

This promotion would have given him an onsite opportunity for 2 years in the UK. I roughly remembered him talking about it before, but at that time, I was preoccupied with my own thoughts. Now, he had missed out on the promotion. Despite working tirelessly to create the pilot project, the company promoted someone else from the team and sent onsite.

I tried to comfort him, saying, It's the nature of corporate life. He needs to learn to adapt. And out of curiosity asked, why was the onsite opportunity so important to him. As he was never motivated by money. Joy answered with a broken voice, 'I thought I would pursue some art training in the UK and, with my savings, open an art gallery here in Bangalore, where I could live my dream on weekends after a hectic work week.'

I understood the pain Joy was going through. I knew what it was like to have a dream but be unable to reach it, and in Joy's case, he was so close. I held him in my arms as tears continued to flow. Eventually, I managed to convince him to go for a walk, hoping that the fresh air outside might help him cope with the betrayal.

As we walked towards the ring road, Joy began to share his feelings. 'Adi,' he started, his voice filled with frustration, 'It feels like my dreams are slipping away. All the hard work and dedication – for what? Someone else gets the opportunity I worked so hard for'.

I wasn't sure how to calm Joy down. I simply said, this setback might be a blessing in disguise. Maybe it's pushing you towards your dream in another way. Let's not let this discourage you; let's turn it into an opportunity.

'But how, Adi?' he asked with frustration in his voice.

I politely asked him to join me in the business. But he was adamant, saying, 'We need money, resources, and a team. I can't see a way forward for your business vision.'

Our discussion delved deeper. I told him that he was wrong. I had been working on this for quite some time. I've got contacts, potential investors, and two guys from the office who are willing to join us in building the product. Together, we can make our dream a reality. We can create something meaningful, something that's ours.

Joy listened to me carefully and looked at me with a glimmer of hope in his tearful eyes.

He asked softly, 'Do you really think we can do it?'

I tried to share my feelings with him, telling him that I believe in us and together we can turn our setbacks into a comeback. Let's build our own path and create our destiny.

In the middle of our disheartening conversation, we decided to drown our sorrows in a beer. We headed to the nearest wine shop with a small sitting area near the road. Our initial plan was to have just one beer and return home since we both had work the next day. Unaware of it, the night in that humble roadside bar, sitting on plastic chairs, would turn the wheel of our destiny. They say, the journey matters more than the destination, and that night, we experienced the pleasure of realising our struggles and our social value."

Adi continued to narrate the story, completely lost in it, while Diya and Tanya patiently listened to the tale of two friends.

"After finishing the second bottle, Joy became very emotional. He started sharing his inner voice, 'I used to think life is good. We are having fun, we have jobs, and society respects us—so-called white-collar employees. But today, I realised we're nothing but well-dressed, English-speaking slaves who can be replaced anytime."

I heard Joy expressing himself in this way for the first time. This topic struck a chord with me, and I couldn't resist adding to it. It's evident in the names themselves—Naukri, Chakri, Service—all derived from slavery. From Naukar to Naukri, Chakar to Chakri, and in English, Servant to Service. Servants never have a say; we need to dance as the master asks.

Joy nodded in agreement, adding, 'So true. That's what happened to me today. Have you seen the movie Madagascar? There, the penguins deploy monkeys to paddle the airship, and to motivate the monkeys, they hang bananas on the top. But it's hung in such a way that when monkeys press the paddle and reach the top, the banana goes even higher.'

I nodded, seeing the similarity to our promotion.

Joy clarified, 'No, it's like our year-end hike. The percentage of hikes we get raises our lifestyles, along with inflation. The promotion is the throttle of the system— when they need more thrust, the penguin doubles the bananas, and the monkeys try to push the paddle even harder to reach the top. Unbeknownst to them, the system is designed in such a way that they'll never be able to reach the banana.'

I couldn't help but agree with the thought. I tried to calm him with my words: that's natural, my friend. If the monkey reaches the banana, they'll eat it and will no longer paddle the wheel. Do you know why corporate offices are so exotic? Because they give you the feeling of being part of the upper class, even though your salary is lower than that of some of the tea vendors. However, your lifestyle expenses are doubled to maintain the false ego that you are an educated, white-collar corporate employee. That's the middle-class trap.

That night, those discussions might have sounded like drunken talk, but every statement rang true; it was like gaining enlightenment in our lives.

We ordered another round of beer and then another; the frustrations and discussions flowed freely like a boat on a river.

And then I saw Joy crying, saying You know, Adi when Ma (Mother) passed away, I was in college doing my engineering. My father had to manage my fees along with Ma's medical expenses. I understand the burden it created on him. Sometimes, he had to negotiate between the expenses of my mother's treatment and the needs of my education. But he never complained, and neither did my Ma. Middle-class parents are like that. And one day, Ma left us. Maybe Baba would have treated her better if he had no burden on my education, and maybe then, Ma would have still been with us.'

I really had no words to console him at that time. He continued, 'And now, after all these sacrifices, what am I giving back to them? My old father is living alone because I had to leave my hometown for a job. I can't send him money because I can hardly save anything from my salary. So, what am I doing? You were correct; this is not life.'

Listening to Joy's words, I, too, underwent self-reflection. I told him about my father. He had a small shop to support our family of 4. I was always a demanding kid, used to fighting with him for my needs, never understanding how he managed to fulfil my demands. But parents being parents, Ma and Baba always supported me and encouraged me to move ahead in life. I have seen poverty, and that's the reason I know there is no novelty in poverty. Society needs slaves, and that's why they teach us to be content, to be happy in poverty, and they present it as morality. As a result, generation after generation, we serve the rich."

Joy agreed with my thoughts, 'I can very well understand now. You know, I love Diya very much. But now, I think, on what basis will she marry me? I have a meagre salary. I know maybe I will earn more with time and experience, but what if she can't wait until then? How will I live after that?'

The discussion of us that night became so intense that we do not recall how many beers we drank and how many drops of tears passed from our eyes. Suddenly, I cannot remember why I felt it was late and that we should go back. So, I asked Joy, it's already very late and we have work tomorrow, come on, let's go back. We can think so much, but in the morning, we have to return to the office to feed ourselves; no choice, buddy.

Then, we paid the bill for the drinks and came out of the bar.

Joy asked me again, 'Adi, are you sure we can make a business?'

I took a deep breath and replied, you know, Joy, when I was in college, our exam syllabus usually consisted of

5 units, each with multiple topics and chapters. All my friends tried to prepare all 5 units, but I could never prepare more than 3 because I used to start from scratch and prepare those 3 units so strongly that I could teach them to anyone if needed... In the exam, out of 5 subjective questions worth 80 marks, I could answer 3. But I answered those 3 with full satisfaction as if I would get full marks. I used to make up stories for the remaining 2. After the exam, I always felt very satisfied, irrespective of whether I passed or failed, because I did the best I could do. So, I learned one thing: if you have the courage to take risks, if you can be honest in your work, and can give your 100%, then whatever the result is, you will feel satisfied inside you. You will feel proud of yourself, and that's everything for me. I want to give my 100%. I want to try. Let's leave the success to luck.

Joy nodded and, for the first time, agreed to join the business that night, 'Okay, then I will also give my 100%. I am with you. Let's do it.'

I held Joy's hand in excitement, and both shouted out loud with full force, Let's do iiiitttt.

We were completely lost in our dream world, and suddenly, someone from the roadside building started shouting, 'Hey, don't make noise at midnight. Go home.'

Joy and I turned our necks up towards the balcony to see the man and burst out laughing.

The man became very angry seeing us laughing at him and started scolding us in the local slang.

Both of us started running towards the PG."

Listening until here, Diya said, "I never knew all these stories. And Joy used to think I could leave him for money. Let me meet him in the evening; I will break his head again."

Tanya, on the other hand, deeply moved by the depth of the thoughts, came closer to Adi, held his hand in hers, and said, with a low voice, "And then?"

Chapter 7

THE PROTOTYPE

Adi looked at the clock; it was almost 5.30 in the evening. "We need to leave for the hospital in sometime. Let's get some rest; I will continue on the way to the hospital."

Tanya and Diya both disagreed with the proposal; they wanted to know everything.

"It's okay; we are relaxing while listening to the story. Please tell me; I want to know" Diya said.

"Tanya added, 'Yes, Adi, please. Now we know the beginning and the current situation. Do not leave us in suspense. Tell us what happened in between. What led you both to these legal issues? How did your idea of an emergency medical service turn into a traditional consulting business? Please tell me."

Adi closed his eyes and started again, "Talking about all those days is like taking a safari in the dense jungle of memory. It's peaceful, interesting, but at times, scary too."

He continued, "So, the next day, I woke up late with a hangover and missed my office. As I opened my eyes, I saw a miracle; Joy had glued a chart paper on the wall and started drawing the app flows on that. As soon as I woke up, he turned back to me and started,

'So, I have tried to create some wireframes for our app. At least it can give us the flow of the use cases. Then we will prepare the architecture.'

I, being a mechanical engineer not familiar with all this lingo, stared at him like a fool. The first thing that came to my mind was, you missed the office too?

But Joy said gladly that he had taken off today. He needed a break and also thought about working on our project.

I was so happy to see my best soldier ready for the battle, but in the next second, I realised that I needed to learn a lot to understand my soldier's strategy.

Anyways, Joy understood that by seeing my face, so he started explaining in the lehman language.

'Well, so we are going to have a mobile application where people will join and create a community to help each other in case of a medical emergency. To understand how the app will work, we need to draw the app screens one by one. Like the first screen is to register in the app, then log in, and then other features. This is called wireframes. You can think of everything a user can do in the app as a use case. Now, think how a civil architect builds a blueprint of a house based on how many bedrooms, bathrooms, or kitchens are required; we will similarly have to create an architecture of how different components of our app will be arranged and connected to each other to create the complete flow.'

Honestly, I was seeing everything double that time; I had a terrible headache, but seeing his energy, I shared a smile and asked him to allow me to get fresh; I will join in 15 minutes.

As he nodded, I rushed to the washroom.

Then I started feeling I might have motivated him too much last night. Now, how to get rid of the hangover? On the other hand, I couldn't get a cup of tea. I told him 15 minutes, but how can I be fresh without morning tea? Anyway, I don't recall when I fell asleep again while thinking all this, sitting on the hot seat. And then, suddenly, I realised Joy was knocking on the door. I woke up again and shouted, give me 10 more minutes, please.

I had no option then, so I jumped into the shower with the toothbrush in my mouth, somehow got freshened up, and came out from the washroom.

Seeing me, Joy started again, 'So, we will build our application on a microservice model. This will give us the flexibility and scalability for future options. Also, it will be easy to maintain the application. After all, it is an emergency application, so it can't go off any time.'

Listening till there, I felt that I needed to interrupt; otherwise, my computer engineering class would continue for the entire day.

I said, well, let me write down all the features for you. Then, you plan for the architecture and flows. If you want, I can call the two guys I have talked about in the evening to join you.

Joy agreed and asked me, 'Then what now?'

Tea! please. I proposed to go out for a cup of tea. I have a bad headache; we can discuss it on the way.

He agreed with my request. We went out of the PG for a tea break. There was a bakery near the PG, so we asked for 2 cups of tea. The shopkeeper, Rama Bhaiya, was well known to us. He said that the fat guy who used to be with us was looking very upset that morning. He had been sitting there since morning, then went towards the main road.

'Is everything all right?' he asked.

We understood he was talking about Anish. I asked Joy if he had talked to him this morning.

Joy replied, 'No,' saying that he had been in the room since morning, working on the project.

I pulled out the phone from my pocket and tried to call him; it kept on ringing, but no answer.

I asked Joy to finish the tea quickly and let's head towards the main road. God knows where this guy went; I knew he was very upset about the job, as it was still on hold.

We finished the tea and rushed towards the main road but couldn't see him, so we thought of walking towards KR Puram station, but again, we had no luck. Both of us kept on calling him, but again, there was no answer. Now we were stressed; he was jobless, depressed, and who knows if he did anything wrong. So, we just ran towards the Mahadevapura bus stop, the last possible place he could go.

As we were approaching the bus stop, we could see him sitting on the footpath. We walked closer and realised he was selling eggs.

We reached him; he was ashamed to see us. I could read it in his eyes; I did not say anything to him, just asked if he had a matchbox. He passed the matchbox to me, I lit up a cigarette with that and sat next to him. Joy took a place nearby on the top of a broken pillar.

Anish started with a low voice, 'I am fed up now, Adi, sitting idle in the room. How long will I waste my parents' money like this? This morning, I saw a guy selling duck eggs near our PG. I bought it from him and am selling it here; almost all sold, the last 10 pieces remaining out of 6 trays.'

I was shattered, not having any words to say. Joy, on the other hand, was listening quietly. But Anish understood our concern and changed his voice as he always does, making fun of himself willingly so that people around him can be happy. He did the same that day, starting with his usual way of speaking,

'You know what, this is a profitable business. I made 60 rupees profit per tray; 5 trays are sold, and if I can sell these 10 pieces, then 360 rupees profit in 2 hours. This is my first earning; I will give you guys a samosa treat in the evening.'

I will not be able to express how proud I felt for him that day. He proved that he had courage and a golden heart. He proved no work is small.

Before he could finish his words, he got a customer who bought all 10 eggs.

Joy smiled and asked him,

'Okay, now let's go. We have a lot of work to do.'

We returned to the PG with our lunch packed, and the discussion started again. I also made a call to the guys who were willing to join us.

I tried to brief the three of us. Joy, along with Suhas and Satya (the new guys), will build the application. Anish and I'll work together to make a list of hospitals and ambulance services. Then, Anish will go to them and share our plan to be a partner. Meanwhile, I'll work on the business plan, revenue model, investor data, and pitch.

The planning looked so promising. It's a feeling, I guess, that cannot be expressed in words. When you trust your target and take the first step toward achieving it, a sense of strength and satisfaction starts flowing in your veins. Perhaps that's why people are willing to risk their entire life savings on their ideas. It's not just about making money; it's about making the dream real. It's about creating a story.

Satya and Suhas visited us in the evening. Joy had an intense discussion with them for hours, most of which was above Anish's and my understanding level. But we sat there like obedient students because we knew that to sell the product, we needed to know as much as possible about it. The discussion ended around 9 at night, and from that day on, we had multiple discussions, meetings, and learnings. Anish went to every corner of Bangalore to talk to every possible ambulance, pathology lab, and medical shopkeeper.

I think we should get ready now; we'll be late," Adi said, breaking the flow of the story.

Diya and Tanya were not ready to stop there. "We still have 10-15 minutes to get ready; please continue," they both said with excitement.

Adi nodded, "Okay. So, then our work continued after office and every weekend. As we made one step of progress, we discovered new challenges. Meanwhile, Anish joined the job that was on hold. It became very challenging for all of us to work on the project after office hours. On top of that, we were doing everything self-paced, so keeping ourselves motivated became really tough. I could see the team starting to break apart, and Satya was the first to quit, saying he couldn't manage the time. We realised this might look easy on paper, but in reality, working with a team of three techies with not much experience and part-time, it seemed impossible for us to even make an MVP.

On the other hand, challenges started coming up in my work areas. I discovered there's already a player in the market with a quite similar service. Also, I first learned that to receive an investment, we need to register our company. There are multiple types of company registration options available, but to take investment from angels, we have to register as a Pvt Ltd or Ltd company first, and for that, we need an address. This was a big challenge for us in arranging the money for the company registration and renting a place for the address.

When we were struggling with these problems, Anish was facing another issue. Since this was a unique idea, none of the vendors were interested in entertaining him, and he didn't have anything to show as the company was only an idea until now."

Adi had a look at his wristwatch and continued again, "So after all these challenges and almost 6 months of struggle, we made a prototype with one or 2 ambulance partners that Anish managed. The prototype was very basic and hardly covered all the major use cases, but our courage was unbeatable. We started approaching investors with that, and here we got into the original field of struggle.

Up until this point, I believed in the concept of wealthy individuals, known as angels, who invest in early-stage businesses based on ideas and products. There are also organisations called venture capitalists that inject money into businesses. However, my optimism took a hit when we began reaching out to investors. Despite sending thousands of emails with presentations and demo videos, we received no replies. Our efforts in chasing investors left the team frustrated. Suhas stopped showing up and avoided most meetings. I realised that if we couldn't make progress soon, our dreams would fall down.

One day, Joy's patience broke too; he asked me, 'Adi, do you think we can really secure an investment?'

I told him that I honestly had no idea, but I was trying to put our best effort into making this possible. I assured him that I wouldn't stop until we achieve success.

Joy responded with a heavy tone, 'I appreciate your courage, but let's face the truth, Adi. People like us often fail in this space. That's why thousands never even try. They may jump into the ocean and swim, but there's no boat to rescue them in their fortune.'

His words were practical, but for me, dreaming means seeing beyond the practicality. I was disturbed by his words, and I responded with anger in my voice. If necessary, I'll build my own boat.

Joy was not able to hold his laughter, he asked me sarcastically, what do I think of myself? He told me

'Do you know why we're not getting calls to even present our product? Because we're average, not from a wealthy background, not from reputed tier-1 colleges with great alumni. We're not from well-connected families. So, if we're so average, how can our future be outstanding?'

His question struck deep in my heart, and I couldn't find a reply. I left the room in silence."

Diya interrupted, "So, you guys didn't secure any investors?"

Adi replied, "Yes, in 6 months, we received only one call from an Angel Investor. We were happy, preparing all night with speeches, covering every possible question."

Tanya asked, "So, what went wrong?"

Adi smiled, "Everything. Our identity, educational background, not having big names in our profiles—everything. The investor rejected us without even seeing our product.

That day, we realised the harsh truth: there's no ready boat for people like us to sail to the land of fortune. Either we had to build our own boat or abandon the dream.

After this incident, we avoided discussing the business for the next couple of months. We immersed ourselves in our office work, spending late hours, and the joyous parties vanished. I could hardly recall when we even had a drink together. Somehow, we all avoided being together to sidestep the topic of our dream project."

Diya stopped Adi here, "I think we need to leave now."

"Yes, that's correct," said Tanya; Adi, too, resonates the same.

Chapter 8

CHAKRAVYUHA

The car rolled out of Adi's apartment as the digital clock on the dashboard blinked 6:30 p.m., the time when day meets night. The sun dipped below the horizon, but its last soft rays were still present in the sky, casting a golden glow that painted the clouds with orange and pink shades. It was a sight straight out of a painting, a masterpiece of nature displayed before their eyes.

The gentle evening breeze was whispering through the open windows, carrying a sweet fragrance of the blossoming trees lining the streets of Bangalore. The branches were adorned with clusters of violet flowers, adding a touch of grace to the enchanting atmosphere.

This moment, known as the magic hour, is one of the favourite times for photographers and videographers, when the sunlight casts a soft, special glow. It occurs twice a day, just before sunrise and sunset, making it perfect for capturing beautiful moments against the backdrop of the sky.

Three of them were enjoying the beautiful sights around them while driving through the empty lanes. It was a moment of serenity, making them feel calm and amazed by the beauty of Mother Nature.

The peaceful vibe of the journey continued until they reached the overcrowded main road of Sarjapur. Here, the scene changed dramatically. The road was choked with a cacophony of cars, bikes, and buses, each competing for space in the congested thoroughfare. There wasn't an inch of space with vehicles inching along in a symphony of honking horns and revving engines. The tranquillity of nature was replaced by the chaos of urban life.

The well-known Bangalore traffic. It's famous for its relentless congestion and endless queues of vehicles. It could turn a short 10kilometre trip into a long, tiresome journey of one or even 2 hours. The air was thick with swirling dust, covering everything in a fine layer of dirt. The chaos of constant honking horns and roaring engines contributed to the cacophony of busy city life.

The peace of mind for Adi, Tanya, and Diya was already damaged and had shifted to frustration and impatience. The three were completely stuck in the pain of the notorious traffic. Their journey slowed down to a crawl, moving at a snail's pace among the sea of vehicles.

Adi closed the window to block out the noise of the traffic. He turned on the air conditioning, hoping to cool down the stifling heat inside the car. Tanya looked at her watch and shared her frustration; the evening rush hour had turned the road into a virtual standstill, and it looked impossible for them to reach on time.

"It's always a nightmare during this time of day," Tanya said, her voice sounding disturbed.

Diya was worried about the delay, so she asked. "How long are we allowed to see Joy?"

Tanya turned to Adi for confirmation. "Until 8.30, right?".

Adi nodded tiredly, feeling the weight of sleepless nights pressing on him. The recent events had left him mentally and physically drained. He could feel his eyes getting heavy, his thoughts slowing down.

Struggling against fatigue, Adi rolled down the window and splashed water on his face, trying to stay awake. Tanya noticed Adi struggling. She asked if Adi wanted her to drive, but Adi was confident.

"I'll be okay," he reassured them.

Diya said with a concerned voice. "Anish messaged. He and uncle reached the hospital."

Adi asked, "Tell them not to wait for us. Uncle must be exhausted and needs to rest."

Diya nodded, getting it. She started to chat to keep Adi awake.

"Why don't you continue the story?" Diya suggested,

Adi's small smile showed he felt better when the conversation moved away from the current problems.

"So, where were we?" he asked, trying to resume the narration.

Tanya recalled the events in order. "You guys had trouble getting funding, and Suhas eventually left the team."

Adi shook his head. "Yes, that dark period," he started his story again with a heavy voice caused by the weight of the memories.

"It was eating me up from the inside. I think the same was happening to Joy as well. After all, he had poured so much of his energy into building the prototype. Anish seemed to be enjoying his job, at least on the surface," Adi reflected.

"But I... I became a completely different person. I found myself sinking into depression. I read over a hundred books just to keep myself busy. I even had to visit a psychiatrist for therapy.

I remember one day I went for my therapy session, and my psychiatrist gave me a great lesson," Adi described, his voice filled with emotion.

"Dr Shah asked about my mental health after a month of medication. I told her I was doing okay, but I was worried about what might happen when I stopped taking the pills. The doctor smiled at me," Adi continued,

"Then she said something I'll never forget. She told me that everyone in the world has a purpose in life, and our whole life is about finding it.

She said, 'success comes to those who know their purpose and use their strengths to achieve it. The others spend their entire lives looking for their purpose and strengths.'

I found comfort in her words, realising that my journey wasn't just about overcoming obstacles, but also about understanding my inner self and my purpose in the world."

Adi's story continues…

"Dr. Shah's words felt like a warm blanket wrapping around me. She told me that I had already taken the first step towards fulfilling my purpose, as I have identified it. Business is my purpose. She encouraged me to enjoy the progress I had made and to prepare myself for the next steps.

And then, the doctor shared another word of wisdom. She told me to always acknowledge my weaknesses, to accept them without shame, and to build defences against them. Only by facing our weaknesses, we can truly overcome them.

That day, I left Dr. Shah's office, with determination, and I felt a new sense of purpose. I understood that it wasn't the end, but the start. All I needed was to take a step back, look at things differently, and find the solutions. After all, there is always a solution to a problem available; we just need to find it.

I got back to the PG, sent a quick email to my manager for a two-week vacation, and started packing my bags. My mind was racing with thoughts as I closed my suitcase. Just then, Joy came back from work; his expression was worth watching that day." Adi smiled while sharing the story

"He asked where I was heading to."

"Home", I replied. I'll be back in 2 weeks".

"Joy's brows furrowed, and he said, 'You could have told me earlier. I would have planned a trip to Indore to visit Baba, too.'

I managed to smile and told him that I only found out 2 hours ago.

His confusion intensified as he asked me, 'What! Are you alright? Is everything fine in Kolkata? '

I'm good, I assured him calmly. Just going home to see Ma and Baba.

Joy's confusion seemed to grow, and he burst out, 'Okay, let me guess, are you going to see a girl for marriage?'

I was taken aback, unsure of how to respond. I laughed and said, No, Yaar, nothing like that. You know marriage is not my cup of tea, anyway.

After completing my packing, I started searching for a flight ticket for the next day. Joy, meanwhile, busied himself with his own tasks. The last-minute flight prices were excessive, some costing even more than my monthly salary. After searching extensively and applying every discount I could find a ticket that fits my pocket for the next afternoon.

Joy returned to the room; he asked, 'So, did you book your flight?'

I nodded yes.

'When?' he asked again.

afternoon flight at 3:30

'Okay, bring some rasgullas on your way back,' he requested."

Adi's sleepiness disappeared as he got into the story. With each word, it was like he was back in those days, his face alive with memories. He kept going with excitement, eager to tell the story...

"Joy wasn't sure about my sudden trip to Kolkata. He passed a cigarette to me, then said, 'Adi, you always used to say we should give our best and then accept whatever happens, right? Well, we've given our best. Let's accept it.'

I accepted it, I replied to him with a smile.

He was not ready to believe me, 'Seeing you every day, I can tell just how much you've been able to accept the fact,' he remarked.

I looked at Joy and said, yes, I have accepted it, but not in the way you're thinking.

Curious, Joy asked, 'Then what?'

I explained to him, there are 2 things we can accept in this situation. One is that no one will finance us, and we do not have enough money or resources. In that case, this idea or business is not for us. We could withdraw from the race altogether. But there's another aspect to consider

Joy asked 'what' In suspense.

To acknowledge our weaknesses and build defences around them, I said.

Naturally, Joy didn't understand the meaning and requested an explanation.

I tried to explain to him that in this world, everyone has strengths and weaknesses. Now, if our ability to innovate or create a business, is our strength, then can you tell me what our weakness is?

Joy requested me to answer the question.

So, I started again: our weakness is our background. This single word carries a lot of weight. We're not from a wealthy family, we lack money, no influential connections, and we didn't attend a tier one college, so we lack the brand to support us. Now, if these are our weaknesses, and we acknowledge them, then we just need to work out a plan to address them.

Joy asked again, 'What does it mean?'

I smiled and replied that because we can't change the truth, the only way to avoid it is to create a diversion in the path of our dreams.

'And how can we do that?'

I don't know, Joy, I admitted. But what I do know now is that we need to find a solution. We need to find a solution for our funding. It's clear that no one is going to invest in our business because, in the initial stages, investors invest in the entrepreneur, and our profile simply doesn't promise success to them.

Joy was very disturbed by my analysis. 'So, after all this analysis, you understand this? What's new in this? Didn't we already know this?'

I replied again, yes, we knew, but we didn't accept it. We were sad because we hoped, and we hoped because we didn't accept the reality. And because we didn't accept reality, we didn't think about mitigation. Please understand the chronology, Joy.

He seemed unsure how to respond to my words. 'Maybe you're trying to tell me something really interesting, but I can't quite grasp it. Or you have really gone mad; it sounds like beating around the bush to me.'

Hmm, I can understand. I'll make you understand once I find a way out of this chakravyuha (circular trap), I assured him. You know, this is the trap, and this is the reason many like us never managed to make it. It's not because they lack ideas or talent.

'Maybe,' Joy answered. 'Anyways, go home, enjoy the trip, have some rest, and then come back with a fresh mind. I can see you need it badly.'

I agreed with a simple hmm and bid him good night."

"So, you went to Kolkata," Tanya interrupted the flow of the story.

"Yes," Adi replied. "The next day, I boarded the flight for Kolkata and landed in the City of Joy with the evening sunset."

Chapter 9

THE REJECTION

Adi had a strong bond with Kolkata. For him, it wasn't just a place on the map; it held many memories and emotions from his childhood. Kolkata kept them safe, like a caring mother preserving her child's toys.

Adi's voice reflected the deep emotions he held for Kolkata as he narrated his story. Returning to the city always brought him comfort. It was like finding peace in the mother's embrace.

Kolkata is called the "City of Joy" because of its vibrant culture, rich history, and lively spirit among its people. It has a unique charm that spreads through the air beyond just personal attachment.

The city has a rich history. It served as the capital of British India until 1911, when the capital moved to New Delhi. Kolkata was established by the British East India Company in the late 17th century with 3 villages: Gobindapur, Sutanuti, and Kalikata. From then on, Kolkata's dominance as a business, cultural and intellectual hub spread all over India.

The strategic location of Kolkata, on the bank of the Hooghly River helped it flourish as a major city in India since the time of the British Empire.

Today, Kolkata stands as a symbol of resilience and progress. The streets here blend with colonial architecture, vibrant markets, and lively festivals like Durga Puja, each of them telling a tale of its past and present. Whether it's the iconic Howrah Bridge or the majestic Victoria Memorial, Kolkata's landmarks reflect its rich history and enduring spirit.

Adi's story continues, while the other two lost in it.

"I booked a taxi home via Eastern Metropolitan Bypass, feeling the city's pulse in the rhythm of the road beneath us. Kolkata's weather was a bit warmer than Bangalore's, but the spring evenings are usually cooler and refreshing. As the cab zoomed along the bypass toward Garia, I felt a sense of renewal washing over me. The burden of past failures and big dreams faded away in the air; my crazy mind could finally feel some peace.

Meanwhile, the taxi stopped at the Patuli signal. I couldn't resist myself and turned to the driver, asking him, Dada (Brother), can you please take a left? Let's pause for a tea break before continuing.

Patuli is a small neighbourhood located in southeastern Kolkata, adjacent to the bypass. This is exactly where I come from," Adi said with excitement.

"Driver Dada happily accepted the proposal for the tea break and turned the wheel left towards the fire station, then took another left, leading us to a renowned tea stall called 'Jeet's Lonka Cha' (Jeet's Chilly Tea). I had a soft spot for this place, especially for its signature spicy tea. The guy there has invented a tea infused with chilli, and trust me, it tastes awesome. With every sip, it's a blend of slightly spicy, salty, mixed with sour flavours; overall, it's hard to describe. Moreover, it's refreshing unlike any other. You should definitely try it," Adi told the girls.

Tanya and Diya replied with excitement, "Sure, the treats are on you."

Adi smiled and continued,

"My house was not far from there; I reached home in around 30 minutes after finishing my tea. My mother was eagerly waiting at the gate. Her happy face at my return surpassed even my own. There's a special kind of happiness that envelops a household when a loved one returns after a long time. My return was no less than a celebration for my mother. Her face was glowing with excitement. It was a feeling that I cannot explain - a mix of relief, love, and a strong bond between us.

The moment brought joy and concern for my parents. They missed me a lot. Now that I'm back home, they're relieved to have me safe with them again. But, like always, they already started worrying about the day I'll have to leave again."

"I freshened up and joined the family for dinner. It had been ages since I tasted my mother's cooking—Alu posto (Potato curry with poppy seed paste), chanar dalna (Indian curry with cottage cheese), and Ruti (Indian flatbread) -Bengali cuisine,a heavenly blend of flavours. Various topics were discussed at the dinner table, ranging from serious ones like elections and politics to light-hearted ones like Bollywood movies.

I was very tired from the trip and made my way to my bedroom. Suddenly, there was a gentle knock at the door. I opened it; it was my mother. She entered quietly and started arranging my bed before taking a seat in the corner. With concern etched on her face, she asked me if I was alright. That day, I realised it's next to impossible to hide your tension from your mother. Mothers have a third eye; they can see their kids' concerns clearly.

Despite my attempts to mask my stress, she could sense the depth of my worries written on my face. However, I couldn't burden her with my troubles; her health was in any way not very stable, and sharing my pain would only cause her distress. With determination, I pushed down my feelings and pretended to be calm, assuring her that everything was okay.

At that moment, I simply wanted to rest my head in her lap, finding comfort in her soothing presence. But being a grown-up creates distance, something that held me back. Maybe I was aware that my gesture could make her more worried.

She called me to sit in front of her, looked at me and reminded me of my roots—an upbringing in a middle-class family in a country of 1.4 billion. Every achievement I had earned until that day was a testament to my strength and determination, a testament to the struggles I faced and overcome. She told me that I am her fighter, capable of withstanding any storm that lay ahead. These were the words I was expecting from her at that time; I knew how her words could do magic on me.

She bade me goodnight and left the room. I said good night to her, filled with gratitude. I felt a sense of empowerment surging within me. That night, my dream transformed into determination, my last resort in life. I felt an inner encouragement, a do-or-die spirit grown inside me."

"The next day after a filling breakfast, I went to see some of my old friends. It was a wonderful day, full of memories and laughter as we talked about the past.

But as the evening came, things took an unexpected turn when Ma surprised me — She told me I would have to go to Durgapur to meet a girl she had chosen for me. Marriage, something I hadn't really thought about, suddenly felt real. Ma thought getting married would make me more responsible and stable in life. But I wasn't sure how to make her understand that I was not ready for it.

I tried to explain to her, but she remained calm yet firm, saying, 'It's okay. I'm not saying you have to get married right away. Just meet the girl for now, and we'll think about marriage later. Or we can do a simple court marriage first, then the ceremony later whenever you're ready.'

I felt confused. What's the difference, I wondered?

Ma explained, sounding a bit frustrated, 'Arranging a marriage takes time. From meeting the girl to setting dates, it's a long process. You're only 25, and she's 23. There's no rush.'

I was not sure what else to do, so with no choice, I agreed to go to Durgapur."

Listening till here, Tanya broke the silence and asked, "So you went for marriage? How was the girl?"

Before Tanya could finish her question, Diya broke out into laughter. Her laughter made Adi and Tanya uneasy.

Adi tried not to focus on the questions he carried on with the story,

"The next day, I took a three-hour bus journey from Esplanade bus stop to Durgapur."

It is a small city in the heart of West Bengal. Durgapur is famous for its steel plant and the Damodar River Valley Corporation. My uncle used to work as a plant engineer at the steel plant, while my aunt kept herself busy managing their home. Their daughter, my beloved sister Anu, is a ray of sunshine in their lives. When I arrived at the city centre bus stop, there she was, waiting with her bicycle, a sight that never failed to bring a smile to my face. But as usual, Anu wasted no time poking fun at me, commenting on my skinny frame and teasing me about my bachelor status. I smiled and tried to ignore her teasing; my mind was focused on something else.

Have you seen the girl? I asked her

Anu did not miss this chance to mock me ruthlessly, 'Oh, so I heard someone does not want to get married!'

I brushed off her teasing, saying that while I wasn't thinking about marriage right away, there was no harm in meeting the girl.

Anu agreed to tell me about the girl, but only if I bought her an ice cream. I laughed at her playfulness, as I wasn't in favour of bribery. However, when she threatened to tell our aunt and uncle about my query., I had no choice but to agree to her condition.

I bought her an ice cream, and we started walking towards Anu's house. She was about to tell me the details of the girl, Shreya. Her phone rang. Anu looked puzzled as she answered and became busy. I had nothing to do but keep on walking, so I started humming to myself, -'Suno na suno na, sun lo na, Humsafar mujhi ko chun lo na,' a Bollywood song, which translates like listen to my appeal, please choose me as your companion, then something unforgettable happened: she put the phone on speaker.

The sweet sound of 'Dil ne tum ko chun liya hai, tum bhee isko chuno na' (The heart has chosen you; you should also choose it.) surprised me. Anu rolled out of laughter and then calmed herself after some time, explaining what happened—It was Shreya on the call with her, and she started singing along when she heard my voice. The meaning of the 2 songs unexpectedly complemented each other. It was as if I had just proposed to her, and she had accepted it. It was a funny moment, and even though I was initially surprised, but was amazed by the coincidence."

"In the afternoon, Aunty made a wonderful lunch for me. She cooked all my favourite dishes, which were perfect traditional Bengali foods, some of which are even hard to find nowadays. We had "Lau Chingri," a dish with bottled gourd and prawns, "Kochur Loti" (taro stolon) with Chola (Bengal gram), "cholar dal with korola (bitter gourd)," Vharali (banana stem), "Doi Katla" (Katla fish cooked with yoghurt), and more. It was such a delicious lunch, and after eating so much, I fell asleep while talking to Anu.

In the evening, my aunt woke me up and asked me to come with her to Shreya's house. Shreya is the daughter of my auntie's friend from when they were kids. They both grew up together in Kolkata and ended up getting married in Durgapur; they've been close for a long time.

I, along with my uncle, Aunt, and Anu, went to their house. I thought the meeting would be formal, like in movies, where the girl wears traditional clothes and offers sweets and Samosas. I would be the centre of attention as the groom. But it was different there. When we rang the bell, a girl in casual clothes opened the door. She was wearing green palazzo pants, a white t-shirt, and a blue scarf; her hair was not properly brushed, and she had no makeup on. At first, I thought she might be the house helper because I was expecting the bride to be in traditional attire. It was all happening for the first time with me. But then, I heard my aunt call her Shreya. I realised how wrong I was; life could be different from movies.

I wondered if they knew I wasn't ready for marriage, but I pushed aside my confusion and followed them into the nicely decorated two-story house. Shreya led us to the living room. Anu and I shared a glance, silently teasing each other while enjoying the moment.

A few moments later, Shreya's mother came out from the attached kitchen, holding a spoon in her hand. She greeted us and asked us to sit while she was frying the puris. My aunt went to join her in the kitchen. Shortly after, Shreya's father came down from upstairs with a whisky bottle.

'All good?' he asked. I replied with a foolish smile, saying, yes, uncle He smiled back and poured 2 glasses of whisky. I thought the evening would be fun now, but I was mistaken—it wasn't for me. He poured one for himself and the other for his friend, my uncle. Neither of them realised that I was left out. Anyway, I didn't mind; I was enjoying the moment. My mind was convincing me that marriage is not too bad, imagining the possibility of having him as my cool father-in-law."

Upon hearing this, Diya poked Tanya, suggesting that they could skip this part of the story. Tanya, feeling a bit disturbed, responded sarcastically, "Me and Adi are nothing more than friends."

Adi, too, took the opportunity to pull Tanya's leg, "I can skip the whole topic if you want."

In response, Tanya playfully pushed Adi and told him to continue with his story,

"The story is better than sitting in traffic and getting bored."

Adi agreed and resumed his narration, "Okay, then let's go back to Durgapur."

"So, Sonali aunty served us puris (deep-fried bread) with dum Alu (Potato Curry) and lots of sweets. She sat with us and started chatting with my aunt."

I noticed the uncles had gone to the balcony, probably to smoke. Suddenly, Sonali aunty suggested that Shreya and I could talk alone, which made me feel a little awkward.

But honestly, I was waiting for this opportunity. She also suggested that we could go to the terrace. My aunty took the opportunity and encouraged me to go ahead.

As we got ready to go to the terrace, Anu tried to come with us, but aunty asked her to stay back to give Shreya and me some privacy. Her expression was priceless at that moment.

Shreya and I went to the terrace, exchanging nervous looks. It was our first meeting, and we weren't sure what to say or how to behave.

I tried to start a conversation by talking about the weather, saying it looked like the clouds were playing hide and seek with the stars tonight.

Shreya smiled. She was a bit relieved by my light-hearted approach. 'Yes, it seems like they're having quite the game up there,' she replied, pointing to the sky.

I wanted to keep the conversation going, so I asked Shreya about her hobbies. So, Shreya, what do you like to do in your free time? Any hidden talents or secret passions?

Shreya became a little comfortable with my friendly attitude. 'Well, I do enjoy painting, though I wouldn't call myself a Picasso just yet,' she joked.

I laughed, appreciating her sense of humour. Who knows? Maybe you'll become the next big artist, and I'll be able to say I knew you when you were just starting out.

We continued talking, sharing stories and laughs as we got to know each other better. Despite the initial awkwardness, we found ourselves enjoying each other's company and looking forward to the future.

But that turned out to be our first and last meeting. The next day, I went back to Kolkata, thinking about whether I should say yes. I genuinely liked Shreya. Her simplicity and bubbly nature touched me from the inside. Everyone was waiting for my answer. I felt pressured but finally made up my mind, yes.

Surprisingly, I found out that Shreya declined the marriage proposal. She wanted to finish her master's degree first, and if things worked out, then maybe she could think about marriage later. It hurt my pride a bit, but I accepted it; at least she prioritised her education. If she had said she didn't like me, Anu and my brother would have teased me endlessly about it.

I never saw or spoke to her again."

Tanya was eager to move on now and suggested returning to the main topic without the usual romantic drama.

Adi glanced at Tanya, teasing her with a funny expression, then continued.

"The 2 weeks of vacation passed quickly, and the next day, I had to catch an early morning flight back to Bangalore. It was always tough leaving home and the beloved city. Saying goodbye was difficult, but the promise of fortune, money, and a career helped bear the pain.

That night, after packing my bags, I joined my parents and brother at the dinner table. We were having dinner and watching a Bengali stand-up comedy show on TV when something remarkable happened."

Tanya and Diya, curious, asked "what had happened."

"There was a joke about government jobs, how thousands of forms are sold for just one position, making more money than the appointee's lifetime salary."

This left both of them confused, and Tanya asked for clarification.

Adi tried to simplify it. He said, "Imagine there are 10 positions available in a government office. They start selling forms for the entrance exam, each costing 1000 rupees. If 5 lakh forms are sold, the total earnings is 50 crores. Now, if the salary for each position is 25 thousand rupees per month, the yearly salary for one person is 3 lakhs. Assuming the salary stays the same until retirement, which is around 35 years, the total lifetime income for one person would be approximately 1 crore 5 lakhs. For 10 positions, it would be 10 crores, 50 lakhs. But the initial income from selling forms is almost 5 times more than the total salary for all the open positions."

Diya was surprised and said, "I never thought like that before. You're right, it's possible."

Tanya chimed in, "But don't forget about inflation. Every year, there is around 6 per cent inflation. So, the government would at least give a 6 per cent minimum increment."

Adi smiled and responded, "The initial earnings are 50 crores, which is already 5 times more than the need. Plus, imagine if you simply put that money in a fixed deposit with 6% growth guaranteed. Other options like stocks, mutual funds, gold, or land are still open for you."

Tanya agreed, saying, "Yes, that can be done."

Adi replied with excitement, "I thought the same! I spent the entire night calculating. This opened the path for our business."

Both Tanya and Diya asked in a confused voice, "But how is this related to your business?"

Adi explained again, "Well, since we couldn't secure funding for our business, a terrible idea popped into my mind. What if we start a company and recruit people based on an exam? We could charge a token amount for the exam, generating a large sum of money. Additionally, we would have a pool of free workers that we could utilise according to our business needs. That was the idea that eventually evolved into today's Soriya Digitech, the IT consulting firm."

"So basically, a shell company," said Tanya.

Adi responded, "Not exactly; there are some more layers to this."

The discussion was ongoing, and the car approached the gate of Oasis Hospital in Whitefield, Bangalore.

Chapter 10

JEENA YAHA MARNA YAHA

Anish and Joy's father left the hospital and headed home. On their way out, they spotted Adi with the girls. Anish waved his hand at them to grab their attention. Adi signalled back from the parking area for them to wait. Quickly, they parked the car and hurried towards the building entrance, where Anish and Joy's father were standing.

Adi looked tired, with red eyes showing his sleepless nights. Diya and Tanya also looked worn out from recent days; their fatigue was reflecting in their expressions. Anish, on the other hand, seemed energetic as usual. He greeted Adi warmly, "Great timing! We were just leaving. Visiting hours are almost over."

Adi expressed regret for the delay and apologised for underestimating the Bangalore traffic. "Sorry, I didn't think it would take this long."

Tanya and Diya also explained the chaotic traffic conditions outside, which had caused them to be this late.

Joy's father encouraged them, saying, "No worries, do not waste time here; go ahead and visit your friend. He's waiting."

"Would you like us to stay?" Anish asked.

Adi denied firmly, "No, please go ahead with uncle and take a rest. I'll arrange a cab for Diya and Tanya and will stay back for the night."

"Visitors aren't permitted to stay overnight," remarked Joy's father. "And Joy has improved a lot now. The doctor mentioned that if his condition remains stable for the next 3 days, they'll release him. So, don't worry. You, too, go home and rest."

Adi nodded silently and went inside.

Inside Joy's room, there was a sense of relief. Though Joy remained connected to his hospital bed by monitors and tubes, he was looking much better.

When Joy saw his friends, he smiled warmly and said, "Sorry, guys, for putting you through this trouble since last night."

Diya responded with a touch of sarcasm, "Oh, no worries, we're having the best time of our lives at the hospital." Then she gently held Joy's hand and said, "If you were aware enough, why did you get excessively drunk and end up here?"

Before Joy could respond, Tanya interrupted, "Let's not fight guys. It was an accident, and accidents happen. But next time, let's try to be more careful."

Adi settled onto a nearby stool, making himself comfortable. "Focus on getting better, and we'll celebrate once you're back on your feet," he remarked.

Agreeing with Adi, both Diya and Tanya smiled, but Joy's expression turned dark.

"What's there to celebrate?" Joy questioned. "Don't forget, we're still on bail. The case is ongoing, and there's a chance we might end up in jail."

Adi took a deep breath and replied with a confident voice, "Do you trust me?"

Without any doubt, Joy replied, "Of course."

"Then keep your faith in me," Adi urged, "This storm is doing nothing but washing away our past sins to pave the path for a brighter future. You'll rise as a respected business leader—I promise."

Though Adi's words resonated with assurance, a flicker of doubt lingered in his eyes. He couldn't hide it from Tanya as they exchanged a glance. Adi quickly averted his gaze, but Tanya could sense the turbulence he was carrying inside. On the other hand, his words helped Joy gain some confidence and brought a faint smile to Diya's face as she looked at Joy with loving eyes.

Joy looked at Diya with a blank face and asked, "Will you try to stay tonight with me, please?"

"Hospital authority doesn't allow overnight visitors, but I'll see if I can arrange something. If not, I'll be back first thing in the morning," Diya assured Joy.

"You know, Joy," Diya said, turning to Adi, "He was telling us all about the tough times you two-faced and how both fought with it to build the company."

Joy, surprised, looked at Adi, "Did you tell them everything?"

Before Adi could answer, Tanya jumped in, "Not everything. We only heard half the story on our way here."

Adi smiled widely and said, "I think Joy's the best person to finish the story."

Hesitant, Joy said, "But Adi?"

"It's okay, Joy," Adi reassured him. "They're like family. We should not hide anything from them."

"Come on, Joy, don't you trust us?" Diya asked.

With no other choice, Joy began, "So, how much do you guys already know?"

Diya replied, "Just until Adi came back to Bangalore with the idea to start the company with people's money."

"Ahh, okay,"… Joy took some time to think, and then he started, "Alright, so the idea sounds simple, but making it happen was not at all an easy task. Those early days were all about figuring out the numbers—how much to charge the candidates, how many candidates to bring on board, and how to reach them. Selling this idea to so many candidates seemed impossible."

Tanya eagerly asked, "So, what did you do?"

Joy continued, "We had to do a lot of homework first. For the initial days, I learned about corporate laws, regulations, and compliances."

"And then the numbers…" Joy took a pause here and asked Adi "why don't you explain the numbers?".

Adi nodded. He started explaining the strategy of the business, "We decided to target smaller colleges, especially non-tech grads interested in software engineering, or dream of having a high paid corporate job. But it wasn't easy. These students didn't have much money, and convincing them to join was tough. So, we kept the job application fee low, at 1500 rupees. It was affordable and less risky for unemployed candidates. If there were any issues later on, not many would complain over 1500 rupees."

"Our goal was to sell 1 lakh job applications, making 15 crores in funding," Adi continued. "The plan was we'd hire 50 people from this 1 lakh pool. Also, it was decided to keep 50% of the 15 crores as running capital, which would be kept as cash at the bank. This would cover 4 to 5 years of salaries for 50 people and 10 management staff, including us, the founders," he pointed at Joy. "Plus, the cash sitting in the bank would earn some interest, which would cover 2 to 3 months of additional salaries every year."

"And what about the remaining 7.5 crores?" Tanya asked.

"The plan was to invest that amount to grow it by at least 9 to 11% annually," Joy explained. "That would give us another 5 years of runway if we don't even do any business. So more or less, the strategy was to keep the company functional for at least 8 to 9 years with one set of recruitment batches, even if we do not have any business."

"And what after 10 years?" Diya wondered.

"That's a risk," Adi reacted quickly. "So, we'd repeat the cycle each year, bringing in a new batch of 50 recruits along with 15 crores in cash. This would keep on increasing the runway."

He took a small pause and started again, "However, my plan wasn't to sustain a bubble forever. I knew it would burst someday. So, we had part of the plan to convert it into a legitimate business—building this workforce with required training and then utilising these free resources to bid for projects from big companies. Our kind of free resource pool would give us the liberty to bid the lowest in the market. That was something that happened; we won multiple big projects, and eventually, our resources got engaged in legitimate projects while the company started earning good profits from the billing for these projects. However, we did not give away our dream; we set up a small team within the company to build our own products. Today, we have 'Get Well Soon,' The product we were not able to arrange funding for is ready to go to market along with 2 different new products."

Diya exclaimed, "Wow, it sounds like a dream! It's like frying the fish with its own fat. Can't even imagine such a plan even working? Two young guys with nothing, living in a PG accommodation, no company, no cash, convinced one lakh people to buy into it?"

"Yes, I had the same doubts initially; who will trust us?" Joy admitted. "But with a solid plan and determination, we pulled it off. And that's why we are facing the Court of Justice now?"

"But how did you do it?" Diya asked again.

Tanya shared the same question; her expression was puzzled.

"Okay, now you know everything. You can decide if we are right or wrong. You might even think we're bad people. But before you judge, think about this: the law says we're cheaters. They're right in a way. We promised people jobs and took their money when we didn't have a business. It seems like a scam, and maybe it is. I get it," Adi said, his voice getting stronger. "But think about the people we hired. Lots of folks in India don't have jobs today. So, what's wrong with giving them a chance? We trained them and got them ready for work. Do you know how many graduates are ready for real jobs? There's a big difference between what they learn and what companies need.

And we didn't just hire our employees. We treated them right. We gave them raises, even though the initial salaries were low, but we provided all the required benefits and paid all the taxes to the government. So, what's the problem? People sometimes need to pay for job applications, right? Sure, we stretched the truth sometimes, but we didn't have any options," Adi said,

The room felt tense. Joy, on the other side, stated softly, "We tried to do things right. We worked hard, built our product, and asked for funding. But nobody even listened to us. We didn't have a chance to demonstrate our product."

"You know why?" Adi's voice was disturbed. He lowered his head, adjusted his glasses and said slowly, "Because we were overlooked, considered ordinary, and meant to be part of the service class. So, we took the challenge and created an army of underdogs whom society never looked at. Today, as these underdogs achieved success, everyone started to hunt us down. His tone turned aggressive and filled with determination, "but we will not run away nor lose the battle. We will win it,"

It didn't take long for Adi to realise that his emotions were getting out of control. He closed his eyes and stayed quiet for some time. The hospital room became completely silent; none of them shared a single word.

Adi started again with a low voice. "I'm not trying to convince you. I just want you to know the truth. My friends and I are fighters. We wanted more than a regular job. Maybe that was a mistake. But I don't think so. We build something new. We helped people find work, acquired and turned around 2 failing companies, invested in startups and won consulting projects from big customers. And now, our company is worth 400 crores. That's the mistake we made."

Adi tried to hold back his tears, his eyes were welling up. Tanya came closer and put her hand on his shoulder. She wiped his tears and hugged him tight.

Silence filled the room again until the nurse entered.

"Visiting time is over. The doctor is coming soon. Please leave so the patient can rest," the nurse said, checking her list of activities.

Adi, Diya, and Tanya had no choice but to say goodnight to Joy.

Diya didn't want to leave Joy alone. She asked the nurse while leaving, "Can I stay with him tonight?"

The nurse disagreed and reminded her of the rule: "Sorry, no visitors at night."

Diya tried to ask again, but the nurse was not willing to listen.

Finally, as negotiation was not an option, they had to leave the room. The three of them walked down the hall, but suddenly Diya said to Adi and Tanya, "You guys go ahead. I'll be back in a minute," and ran back to Joy's room. The nurse was about to say something, but Diya ignored her and sat on the bed next to Joy. She held his hand. Tears filled her eyes as she said, "I'm sorry, Joy. I didn't understand. Life isn't easy, and sometimes we have to do things differently. But I forgot that family and friends should stick together, no matter what."

The nurse saw the couple in their emotional moment, so she decided to give them a few more minutes. "I'll bring dinner in 5 minutes. Please, madam, leave by then," she said and left.

Diya wiped her tears, but she was not finished with her words yet. She continued, "You know, Joy, I don't remember my dad. I don't know why my parents divorced. I've always felt like I missed something in life. There was always a vacuum, maybe because of my dad. I don't want to miss you too. I'll be with you, no matter what. I love you."

Diya's words touched Joy deeply, and he couldn't hold back. He pulled Diya into his arms. Diya rested her head on his chest; her breath started matching with the rhythm of his heartbeat. Diya found ultimate peace here in Joy's arms after the stressful day. Joy lifted her face and placed his lips on her forehead. It was a kiss of togetherness, a promise to be with each other forever. The bond they shared, where love was not dependent on words, could be conveyed through a small kiss to the beloved."

Joy firmly said in her ear while arranging her long hair, "I won't let you down. I'll face whatever happens. I love you too, Diya."

"Time's up, madam," the nurse said, interrupting the intimate moment. She arrived with Joy's dinner.

Diya looked at her, her eyes expressing gratitude and agreement.

She stood up, said goodbye to Joy, and left the cabin.

Adi, Diya, and Tanya stepped out of the hospital. Tanya unknowingly held Adi's hand while Diya looked refreshed, softly humming a song. Their faces were no longer dull; they felt a sense of togetherness and happiness, replacing the ongoing drama in their lives.

"Sometimes sharing our stories with those closest to us brings immense peace of mind," Adi remarked.

"Absolutely," agreed Diya.

As they got into the car, Adi took the driver's seat. It wasn't late yet, and Bangalore's traffic showed no sign of slowing down. But now, they didn't mind. They navigated through the slow-moving traffic like a small boat riding the gentle currents of a steady river. Adi turned on the radio, and to their surprise, the song playing was "Jeena Yahan Marna Yahan…Iske Siva Jana Kahan" - a perfect match for the situation they found themselves in. Life is like a circus, and the show must go on with us as performers and our companions by our side.

Diya rolled down the window, feeling the soft caress of the breeze and letting it play with her hair. Tanya unconsciously began to hum along with the melodious voice of Mukesh. Eventually, Adi joined in too. Their voices blended into a symphony, sending a message to destiny that they weren't defeated yet - they were together.

The car navigated through the busy streets and turned into a narrow alley. A few metres away, Adi hit the brakes, and they arrived at Diya's apartment. Diya stepped out of the car, bidding Adi and Tanya goodnight before disappearing into her apartment.

Adi and Tanya then made a U-turn toward Sarjapur. The road was relatively empty now, and Adi pressed down on the accelerator, eager to reach home.

Chapter 11

TANYA

Adi and Tanya finished their dinner and settled into the sofa. It was so relaxing after such a stressful day. Though it was not over yet, a round trip to the hospital would continue until Joy's discharge.

Tanya decided to stay back with Adi tonight. She wanted to be with him as much as possible in this stressful situation. Anyway, it was quite common for them to stay back in one another's place. Their relationship was more than a simple friendship or just a hookup. Over the years, they had grown closer and closer, their connection deepening with each passing day. But these two were yet to understand that emotion. Both of them were very practical and ambitious. They felt for each other but were afraid to display their emotions. And that's why their relationship as so-called friends did not move ahead to the next stage.

Adi and Tanya found comfort and strength in each other's presence, their companionship blossoming into a source of unwavering support. They settled into their favourite couch, and the cosiness of their bond spread, making the room feel calm and happy. They cherished the peaceful moments together, feeling content just being near each other as they spent another night together.

Their story began in Kolkata during their school days but truly blossomed in Bangalore. They crossed paths again at Phoenix Mall after many years since their last meeting. Destiny seemed to be writing a new chapter for these two souls that day.

It was Tanya's birthday. She and her boyfriend, Akash, went to the mall for shopping and then planned to have some drinks at one of the pubs there.

Adi still remembered the lively evening at Phoenix Mall. It was a crowd-pleasing Friday evening, bustling with people and filled with a pleasant buzz. Adi and Joy were there full of excitement; that was the day they registered their company. It was a moment to relax after a long, hectic day and to celebrate the birth of 'Soriya Digitech' with some chilled Budweiser. So, they found the table on the balcony of Social, a popular pub in the middle of the lively vibrancy of the mall.

Adi and Joy were fully engaged in their discussions when suddenly, a voice full of energy called out from another corner of the balcony, disrupting the rhythm of their conversation. "Aditya Chowdhury?" the voice shouted with excitement, drawing Adi's gaze towards its source.

"Adi looked back when he heard his name. It was Tanya, sitting at the far end of the balcony, waving her hand with a big smile. As their eyes met, it felt like time paused. It was a long-awaited reunion, a surprise meeting that would shape their future unexpectedly. Adi could see little Tanya with a cute smile, waving her double ponytail in the air. The sight of Tanya ignited a spark of nostalgia in him, transporting Adi back to their school days when they had been classmates. He remembered her as the lively new girl with a beautiful voice, often singing at school events, while Adi was a fan of her voice."

Tanya was a lovely girl, not tall; she could be counted among those of shorter stature. She had dusky skin with dense, curly hair. Her bubbly appearance, mixed with a mature attitude, was something Adi always liked. Tanya was never into much fashion; she was wearing simple denim shorts with a baggy white t-shirt, which had a quote written on it: "Do not stare." Her dense, curly hair made her head look even bigger; the hairs untied and out of her control, playing with the air. She wore red lipstick and black-framed glasses, which enhanced her adorable look, while a nose ring added a touch of wildness to her face.

Tanya left her seat and came to Adi's table; she forwarded her hand for a shake and said, "Hello, Adi, how are you? After such a long time, man. I cannot believe we met again; what a coincidence."

Their conversation began and grew increasingly intense, completely forgetting about their companions. The conversation drifted down to the memory lane, recalling incidents from their school days. They recalled their favourite teachers and the quirky nicknames students used to call them. Meanwhile, Tanya's boyfriend, Akash, joined the table with a warm smile, unaware of the invisible connection forming between his girlfriend and Adi.

They were not aware that the meeting would start a new journey filled with laughter, tears, and everything in between. It was destiny bringing them together, two souls destined to find comfort and friendship in each other's company.

From that moment on, Adi and Tanya's friendship bloomed, going beyond the limits of time and space. They grew closer with each passing day, becoming more than just old-school friends. They shared their thoughts, fears, and dreams, supporting each other silently.

After a few months, Tanya broke up with Akash and started to spend more time with Adi, their bond grew stronger, becoming a source of comfort and strength. They found peace in each other's company; their connection evolved into something deeper. Their relationship was easy and natural, without any need for pretence or expectations. They embraced the simplicity of their friendship, finding happiness in being together.

For Adi and Tanya, their relationship was a comfort nest in between life's complexities, a place where they could be themselves without fear. They cherished every moment, feeling grateful for the special bond they shared.

As the night got darker, they cuddled up, feeling peaceful after a busy day. Adi broke the silence with a question, stirring the memories. "Tani, do you remember your first day at our school?"

Tanya's voice was soft against Adi's chest, "Yes, I do. I was so upset on that day."

Hmm, I can remember, but what was the reason?" Adi asked while tracing patterns in Taniya's palm with his finger.

"Arre, it was my first day in a new school after moving to the city, leaving my friends behind.," Taniya replied

Adi nodded, "Yes, it must have been tough. But sometimes changes bring new opportunities to explore, meet new people, and experience different things."

Tanya agreed, "True, but saying goodbye to friends every few years was hard."

Adi exchanged a naughty smile, "But it brought us together."

Adi leaned in, kissing Taniya, while Taniya playfully pushed him, saying, "Let's sleep now. You need rest. You've hardly slept in the last few days."

"Adi didn't want to sleep just yet. He gently flipped Tanya onto the couch and began kissing her passionately, igniting an intense moment between them. The room grew dim as they lost themselves in each other's embrace."

After a long love fight, as they lay together in the soft light of the lamp, Adi lit up a cigarette. He took a few puffs and then asked Tanya, "Should we give our relationship a name?"

Tanya smiled, lifted her head from Adi's arms, took a puff from his cigarette, and then said softly, "What's the point of labels, Adi?"

Adi chuckled, "Yeah, what's the point?"

Tanya teased, "We don't need a label to define us. We're close because we want to be, without any pressure. We understand each other without words, living in the moment."

Adi's tone softened, "Will you be with me forever, Tani?"

Tanya laughed, "What's happened to you today? Of course, I'm with you. We are so engaged with each other that we hardly have time to meet new people anyway."

Adi grinned playfully, "So, should we just go with the flow?"

Tanya took the cigarette again and smashed it in the ashtray, then climbed on top of Adi, a mischievous glint in her eyes. They disappeared again into the darkness, their laughter mixed with whispers of love, filling the room with warmth.

Suddenly, Adi's phone buzzed, breaking the moment.

"Who's interrupting us now?" Tanya asked, sounding a bit annoyed.

Adi glanced at his phone, a smile spreading across his face as he saw a new email from Berlin Equity Partners. However, He decided to ignore it for now and to focus on Tanya.

Tanya, now serious, urged him to pay attention.

Adi replied with a smile, "Yes, Madam, fully present and at your service."

❖ ❖ ❖

Chapter 12

THE WAR OF NARRATIVES

Joy was released from the hospital after a week of admission. It had been weeks since Adi and Joy were arrested by the police. During this time, Soriya Digitech had been struggling with the worst period in its history since its inception.

Initially, there were constant raids by investigating agencies and periodic interrogations of employees. After the arrest of the founder, public sentiment towards the company and its associates became very negative. Employees were so anxious that they even stopped wearing company ID cards in public. Customers were losing confidence in the company's commitments. Some even considered switching to other suppliers. Adding to all these, the media played a significant role in tarnishing the company's image in the public eye. Regular news coverage, debates, the outcry of social workers, and even political involvement exacerbated the situation for the company.

The narrative spread as Soriya Digitech, a shell company that had committed a scam involving crores, with innocent young students as victims. The founders were portrayed as villains of society, having committed the most inhumane crime by cheating poor students and selling them false hopes of a job.

A company, after all, is built on trust—a trust that customers will get value for their money and employees will have a secure future in an ethical environment. Perhaps that's why it's called an organisation, where commitments, values, trust, and morality are organised in a meaningful way that can be believed by all stakeholders.

Today, Adi and Joy headed to the office, but it was no longer the familiar place it used to be. Over 300 pairs of eyes were on them, wondering about the company's fate in the uncertain circumstances. Will the court order to shut down the company? If so, these employees would suddenly become jobless, feeling cheated, recalling the promises made during recruitment. Customers, too, might express their anger, resorting to legal action and complaints, further complicating matters.

Adi reached out to some of the contacts he had cultivated over the years, anticipating such a situation. He called Daina from the famous corporate magazine 'Their Story,' Sudha, the renowned YouTuber, and a few other influencers, invited them to the office at 5 p.m. Additionally, he asked the HR head, Avanti, to schedule a town hall meeting with all employees at 3 p.m. His plan was clear—to address the concerns internally first, then present a united front to the press.

Adi and Joy entered the office floor and made their way to the conference hall, employees stood up, their eyes filled with questions and complaints. Some teased them from the crowd, mocking them as cheaters. Joy felt a bit nervous, but Adi appeared strong and confident. He stopped in the centre of the floor, climbed onto a desk, and spoke loudly:

"This is an office, not a court. If you have any complaints, you're free to file them with the police. But before that, remember one thing: there's a difference between allegations and truth. You are employees of this company, not ours," he said, pointing to Joy.

He continued with a strong voice, "Being loyal to the company is our duty, and that applies to all of us standing under this roof today. Soriya Digitech has taken care of us since its inception, fulfilled our needs, and recognised our capabilities. It has supported each and every one of us. Now, just because some idiot filed a PIL against the company, does it mean we'll lose our trust in the company? We are a family; we always have been and always will be. Together, we've weathered stronger storms than this, and I trust that as a team, we will survive this as well."

Adi paused, locking eyes with each person in the floor. Suddenly, a single clap echoed through the crowd, the sound of 2 hands striking together, igniting a spark—a spark of trust and unity, a gesture of recognition. Soon, applause rippled through the room. Adi nodded to Avanti, signalling her to announce the town hall. Avanti stepped forward and renounced the evening's town hall. She emphasised the company's commitment towards its employees and its transparent culture.

Adi and Joy made their way to the conference room, accompanied by the key executives. The atmosphere was heavy in the room. Adi tried to break the ice, saying, "How's everyone holding up? Looks like our company is getting a lot of attention. We're all over the news. Maybe we should throw a party for our sudden fame," he joked.

However, the joke fell flat, leaving the room silent and sombre. Adi sensed the mood and swiftly transitioned into the role of a strong and humble leader; carefully choosing his words, he said, "Okay, let's get straight to the point. I can understand what's on everyone's minds, but dwelling on it won't help us move forward. As I mentioned outside, we're more than just colleagues—we're a family, a Soriya Digitech family. Yes, the times are tough, but now more than ever, we need to be united to save our company—for the sake of ourselves and our families. So, let's face our challenges head-on. Let's identify them, find the roots, and then prepare a strategy to mitigate or resolve them."

Gradually, the atmosphere started to lighten, creating a more conducive working environment as people began to gain confidence in Adi's leadership. Smiles and nods of agreement filled the room. Adi requested Joy to identify issues concerning customers and deliveries while he assumed the role of a keen listener and started to take notes in his notepad.

Joy listed down each problem on the whiteboard and facilitated brainstorming sessions to find solutions. The meeting was incredibly productive, boiling down numerous worries into 4 key areas: public perception, employee trust, customer confidence, and compliance.

Now breaking his silence, Adi addressed the group again, "Now that we've pinpointed the major problem areas, let's address them systematically. Our public image is the most volatile area. Allegations led to a narrative portraying us as an organisation exploiting youth from middle-class or poor families, playing with their emotions and finances. However, the good part is narratives can be altered, and perceptions can be crafted."

He continued, "The media has used keywords like 'youth,' 'middle-class,' 'poor,' 'cheating,' and 'scam' to grab public attention. That's their job, serving it up like breakfast to people, which they always do. Unfortunately, it seems we've become the news this time. However, it's not all bad. Any publicity is good publicity. Companies spend a fortune to get the level of publicity we've received. Now, our task is to divert this publicity and shape a positive image for ourselves. Ravi (head of marketing) and I will work on this. People often don't think much before consuming news; they form images based on what they see and hear. We're social creatures, often following the crowd without realising which side we're on. So, we'll make our side of the story visible and make it look like a crowd. Ravi will market it and shift public sentiment in our favour."

Turning to Joy, Adi said, "You'll work with Dinesh (head of customer success and sales). Talk to each and every customer, show them our perspective, gain their confidence, and reinstall their trust."

Adi continued, "We have the town hall sometime, and hopefully, our employees will stand with us. Finally, Ramesh (Head of Finance), please connect with the legal team and figure out how to unfreeze our accounts, at least enough to manage expenses and salaries."

The energy of the room charged with purpose and determination; each member absorbed their individual mission with newfound clarity. They understood the weight of the moment as Adi's words made a place in their mind, carrying a sense of conviction and possibility. In times of such difficulty, they learned that with belief, vision, and guidance, any problem can be overcome. The team stood united, prepared to face challenges confidently, driven by the unwavering belief that within every problem lay a solution waiting to be uncovered. No problem is so big that it doesn't have a solution.

As scheduled, the journalists showed up in the afternoon. Adi and Joy respectfully addressed them, going over the details of where one person put 350 futures at risk. They shared their success in helping people find jobs, aiming to convince the media of their positive impact.

Following the press briefing, it was time for the town hall meeting to build trust among employees. At one end of the floor, there was a podium with Soriya Digitech branding, where Adi and Joy used to address their employees. It held many memories of success and achievements, but it was different today. Avanti led the event, explaining the agenda of the meeting and setting the stage for Adi and Joy.

Adi began with the familiar greeting, "Hello, my dear family, how are you?"

He acknowledged the challenging circumstances they were facing, affirming, "Tough times make people strong. They fostered bonds and trust within the family." Feeling the need to unite in tough times, Adi hinted at finding common ground, knowing that people tend to come together when facing challenges while sidelining those who disagree.

After the speech, Adi handed the mic to Joy, knowing Joy wasn't comfortable with such situations. Joy, a technical expert with a creative mind, quickly moved to the Q&A part, welcoming questions from the audience.

One of the employees asked a key question about the company's future if there were ongoing legal issues. Adi jumped in, understanding how important the question was for boosting employee morale. He explained the company's legal setup and financial strength, assuring everyone that Soriya Digitech was not solely dependent on its founders. "The company is stable, and will remain as such". He also talked about the company's dedication to innovation and ethical business practices.

The Q&A session strengthened the employees' trust in Adi and Joy's leadership, making them feel secure and stable during uncertain times.

Next, it was time to set the narrative; Adi was prepared with his plan. Daina and Sudha arrived promptly at 5 o'clock, followed by several online influencers, some of whom were there due to financial arrangements. The office cafeteria transformed into a makeshift interview set for Adi and Joy.

The interview began on a light-hearted note with a gentle introduction of the two young entrepreneurs, Aditya Chowdhury and Joybrata Ganguly.

Daina posed the first question: "So Joy, as we know, you always aspired to be a painter. How did you transition into entrepreneurship?"

Joy smiled and replied, "Honestly, even today, I still have to look up the spelling of 'entrepreneur' – such a challenging word. I would prefer to be known as an inventor. Along with Adi and our brilliant team, we've invented some fascinating products, a few of which are already live while others are set to be launched. I believe these products will simplify life for many."

Next, Sudha, the renowned YouTuber, took the floor. "What's your response to the allegations of looting public money through a recruitment scam?"

Adi seized the moment he had been waiting for. "Allow me," he interjected. "If we've looted, then schools are robbing students by charging fees."

"Could you please elaborate?" inquired Sudha.

"Definitely," Adi continued. "We reached out to students, especially those from tier 2 or 3 colleges and non-technical backgrounds, often overlooked by big companies. It's tough for them to land corporate jobs. They're usually not hired by big recruiting firms and often pursue further education like Master's degrees. We hired them, arranged training, and now they're successful IT engineers. We found a way for people to invest modest fees to create job opportunities. We've proven it works. If charging exam fees is wrong, then I'm guilty. But think about it: is exam preparation really free? As a businessman, I collected fees and provided the promised service. Those who passed are now our employees. What's wrong with that?"

Adi's explanation was thorough yet intentional, aimed at crafting a narrative highlighting that he and Joy had pioneered a new approach to creating employment options for people.

Their message resonated, and the interview ended positively. Adi quietly asked some influencers to turn parts of it into short motivational videos, showing them as resilient figures overcoming challenges to build an empire with innovation and integrity.

Their plan worked. Soon, Adi and Joy became hot topics in the media, especially online, and were seen as heroes. They were being compared with big names in the business world. In just a week's time, the whole story around them changed. They went from being accused of scamming to being seen as smart innovators. With paid influencers backing them, others started creating videos about their story, making it viral. Adi and Joy were praised as pioneering businessmen, famous entrepreneurs, symbols of resilience, and examples of middle-class success. Criticism turned toward the person who filed the case against the company, blaming the biases of the system where instead of thousands of crores of frauds, everyone is behind this little money.

Adi and Joy intentionally skipped the final court hearing. They claimed health issues and attempted to delay the proceedings as they sensed things were going their way. The court agreed to another hearing in a week but banned them from talking to the media or content creators as the public prosecutors accused them of trying to manipulate the case.

Public opinion had shifted heavily in Adi and Joy's favour, like a tidal wave. Seeing this, the court accepted the prosecutor's argument and added another charge: 'attempt to influence public opinion during the trial.'

Despite the legal hurdles, Adi remained optimistic, carefully planning his strategies and keeping his best move for the right time. Meanwhile, Joy recovered fully from his accident, ironically gaining more sympathy for their cause and showcasing the struggles of innovation in the face of opposition.

Chapter 13

PUBLIC INTEREST LITIGATION

It started with a Public Interest Litigation (PIL) filed by a public prosecutor from the Bangalore High Court, backed by a former Soriya Digitech employee, Rajiv Chopra. PILs are legal actions initiated by individuals or organisations to address issues of public interest through the court system. The court then examines those claims, and in the case of acceptance of the appeal, the proceeding starts, followed by the investigation. This PIL accused Soriya Digitech of serious wrongdoing, like running a fake company, engaging in deceptive practices, engaging in fraudulent recruitment, and manipulating court proceedings.

Soriya Digitech Pvt. Ltd. had become the epicentre of this legal storm. The company was established as an IT consulting firm 4 years ago with the aim of providing training, consulting, and knowledge processing services, primarily targeting large businesses. Aditya Chowdhury and Joyabrata Ganguly, the company's founders and directors, each held 45% of the company's shares. The remaining 10% had been distributed among key employees as part of an Employee Stock Ownership Plan (ESOP).

ESOPs are a common strategy among early-stage companies to attract talent without breaking the bank. Under this scheme, employees receive a percentage of share ownership. This can be cashed in upon the company's listing on the stock market or acquisition by a larger entity. Sometimes, the company itself may grow to a point where it buys back ESOP shares from its employees, providing them with substantial financial gains.

The concept of ESOP worked for Soriya Digitech as well and helped the company attract great talents for its growth. Rajiv Chopra was one of them. He was a highly qualified, experienced business leader. Rajiv joined the company as a Business Development Head. He received one percent ESOP along with his salary.

Rajiv was an intelligent and seasoned player in the business world. It did not take much time for him to understand Adi's plans. He studied the company's history to know it well but then used this knowledge for his evil intentions.

One day, Rajiv came to Adi's cabin with an unusual attitude.

"Hello, Rajiv, good morning. Anything wrong?" Adi asked.

Rajiv replied with a smile, "No, man, all good. I came to show my gratitude to you."

Adi was shocked. "Sorry, I did not understand."

"Mr. Aditya Chowdhury, you are a marketing genius. You sold an ordinary recorded course video that might be copied from YouTube to lakhs of people, raising 60 crores? Oh my God, I cannot believe it. I should not call myself a marketing graduate anymore."

Adi sensed what Rajiv was talking about. He controlled himself and chose his words carefully. "Thanks for your appreciation. Indeed, selling to lakhs of people was not an easy task. But the quality of our course material and the demand for jobs in the Indian market helped us, you know."

Seeing Adi so composed, Rajiv became disturbed. His plan to make Adi panic was not working.

"Content my foot; you are a liar, Mr. Chowdhury. Your course is nothing but a power point presentation converted to a video, which is a copy of contents easily available on the Internet for free. It sold because you sold the job application, not the course. People had to buy the course to apply for the job," said Angry Rajiv.

Adi, keeping himself calm, replied, "So, do you see any problem with that?"

"No, and that's why I complimented you as Guinness. The job applications for no job, wow," said Rajiv sarcastically.

Now Adi understood he needed to be straightforward. "What do you want to say?" he asked.

Rajiv continued, "Please understand that I know all your games. How did you build shell companies, market them to people, and earn a lot of money? Companies make products to sell; you made the company a product."

"Okay, I do not need to prove anything to you," said Adi with a strong voice. "Tell me what you want."

"Nothing much, promote me as a director and give me 10% of the company," said Rajiv.

"Are you blackmailing me? Bloody ..." shouted Adi at the top of his voice.

"Not really; I am trying to offer you a deal," Rajiv replied calmly. "You have all the right to say no. However, I, too, have all the right to make this story public. And then, you know, our Indian people are very emotional. I cannot imagine what they will do with a cheater who cheated unemployed young stars."

"Enough is enough." Adi punched the table with all his strength, his voice at its peak. "Do not cross your limit."

Adi wanted to say something more, but he controlled himself. Rajiv on the other side, was calm, A slight smile curved his lips; things were going as he planned.

Adi started again after a few minutes of silence. "I cannot promise anything now. I will talk to Joy and let you know if anything can be done. Meanwhile, keep your mouth shut."

"Okay, I will wait," Rajiv shared a wicked smile and left the cabin.

Adi knew he had to face this eventually, but he never thought his employees would discover his secrets and use them to blackmail him.

He immediately picked up the phone and called Joy.

"Hello, Joy. Can you please come to my cabin now?"

Joy rushed to Adi's cabin in a minute. "What happened, Adi?" Joy asked with a voice full of concern.

Adi, using a couple of slang, said with rage in his voice, "That guy is blackmailing us."

Joy was shocked, as he had no clue what was happening.

Joy calmed Adi and heard the whole story, then said, "Adi, I do not think we should fight with him. Let's give him 10% and keep him under control."

Adi was silent; something started cooking in his mind. This was the strength of Adi. When things go completely out of hand, people start to panic, become aggressive, or break down. Adi was not exceptional, but he could control himself very fast. He started thinking deeply about what had happened and what worse could happen to prepare a strategy around it.

Knowing Adi, Joy understood the analysis going on in his mind. Silence filled the room completely.

Joy broke the awkward silence. "Will you tell me what's going on in your mind?" he asked.

Adi looked at him with a blank face for some time and said, "Let him do whatever he can. We have strong boundaries in all our dealings and transactions. Proving anything will not be easy for him, and anyway, one day, we will have to face these questions."

Joy, with an uneasy voice, said, "No, Adi. If things can be managed internally, why do you want to fight?"

There was logic in Joy's voice, Adi realised. A businessman's mind should never be overtaken by emotion. Every decision should be made in favour of the future.

"We are very close to attracting a big investment and returning all the money we have gathered so far from candidates, even with interest, so there will be no chance of facing any problems in the future," said Joy

Adi agreed, "But I am not sure about his attitude," he said, his voice mixed with doubt and uncertainty."

"We can manage him," Joy replied confidently.

"Well, we have to, but I feel he will create more problems for the company," Adi said.

"We will deal with that when the time comes, Adi. Anyways, he will only have 10%, and we will be in the deciding position," added Joy.

Adi's concern for Rajiv was not misplaced. As they agreed to Rajiv's conditions, his attitude changed. He started behaving rudely with the employees. Adi and Joy treat every employee as family, knowing that they are the company's greatest asset. But Rajiv, not aware of the art of leadership, started acting like a boss.

Meanwhile, an incident occurred that shattered the stability of the company. A female employee lodged a complaint against Rajiv, alleging that he attempted to take advantage of her. HR brought this serious issue to the attention of the founders. Adi & Joy understood the seriousness of the issue, and also it had the potential to attract external attention, including police investigation. They listened attentively to the details and requested HR to escort the employee to their cabin for a discussion before taking any action.

As soon as HR left the cabin, Adi began with frustration, "I knew this would happen. It's not about the 10% share. Rajiv isn't someone who can run a business. He is power-hungry and could single-handedly destroy any company if we give him freedom."

Joy had no answer to this argument and chose to remain silent.

"What do we do now, Joy?" Adi asked.

Joy replied hesitantly, "I do not know. If we take action against him, he may go public with the company's secrets. But if we don't, it will be an injustice to the girl. Also, she may go to the police, which wouldn't be good for us."

While they were discussing, HR knocked on the door and entered with the employee.

Joy offered her a seat and asked if she was comfortable sharing what had happened.

The lady named Monalisa was brave. She explained that Rajiv always tried to touch her whenever he got the chance. On that day, he said, "I am going to be the director of the company, and I can promote you as Business Development Head only if you keep me happy."

Both founders became very angry listening till here.

Adi passed a glass of water to Monalisa and said, "Monalisa, we are sorry for what you had to go through here in the organisation. We promise you that this is a non-negotiable issue for the company. We will take the maximum possible action on this. Please let us know if you have any issues while working here. Feel at home. We are a family here, and people like Rajiv do not have a place in this family."

Adi and Joy had no choice but to fire Rajiv now; things were out of hand. Adi's assumption about Rajiv proved correct. The incident left them in a position where they had to think from the heart. The two young founders were ready to take risks for the business but were not willing to negotiate with this type of behaviour in the workplace. This was not what they dreamed about for their company. If they couldn't even protect their employees within the office, then there was no point in building such organisation.

A few months after this incident, the storm began. Soriya Digitech received a summons from the High Court. A lawyer named Chandrababu Reddy filed a PIL against the company, with Rajiv as his prime witness.

Chapter 14

THE STRATEGY

Rajiv Chopra was the mastermind behind the conspiracy against the brainchild of Adi and Joy. After being fired from the company, he started this game to destroy Soriya Digitech. The dream they passionately pursued, worked tirelessly day and night to build it brick by brick with their dedication, now seemed threatened.

Adi still recalls how challenging it was to navigate every step to reach this point. The memories remain vivid for him, especially the uncertainty of not knowing how to start a company and what type of company to establish. There were numerous options available for registering a company, ranging from sole proprietorship to limited liability and various others. Each type of registration had its own requirements, benefits, and drawbacks. Additionally, there were legal procedures for trademark setup, taxation, and compliance. For Adi and Joy, all of this was more complex than finding a business solution. An entrepreneur must grasp these concepts well and carefully choose each option in alignment with future plans and the nature of the business.

Their vision was clear: to recruit one hundred thousand candidates, each paying a small fee in exchange for job opportunities in the growing IT sector. However, turning it into reality proved extremely difficult. Gaining the trust of potential candidates and figuring out all the complicated rules to start a company was really hard.

Adi, Joy, and Anish worked hard. They spend many hours studying company laws and gathering paperwork. Their path was full of challenges, but they kept going, fuelled by their strong desire to make their dream a reality.

In the middle of those challenging days, Anish remembered his friend Vijay. Vijay was a company secretary who knew a lot about company matters. He was working at a reputable law firm during that time. Anish asked him for help, and Vijay didn't hesitate. He came to the Happy PG to offer his guidance.

Vijay took a seat comfortably on a stool next to Adi's bed. His attitude was helpful yet professional. He quickly laid out a clear plan without any delay. "I've got an hour before I need to go. Ask me anything you need," he said firmly. His calm and confident appearance put Adi, Joy, and Anish at ease, encouraging them to share their doubts and seek clarification.

Joy shared their plan to establish a company and asked for guidance on the process. "What type of company do you have in mind?" Vijay asked.

Before Joy could respond, Adi answered, "Our plan is to set up a training institute with the potential for consultancy services for corporate clients."

Vijay wanted to know if they had a plan to seek investment for this venture, to which they replied yes.

Anish raised another concern, "How can we even establish a company without initial investment? It's needed anyway."

Slightly taken aback, Vijay explained, "You must first set up the company before seeking investment against its shares."

Adi then inquired about the financial requirements for setting up the company."

"Well, since you want to raise future investment, I suggest setting up a private limited company," Vijay advised. "It's a separate legal entity and needs at least 2 shareholders but can have up to 200. Ownership is through shares, which can be sold with some limits. This way, you can use the company's shares to get funding later on."

"What exactly are shares? Can you break it down for us?" Adi inquired, seeking clarification.

Vijay responded with a reassuring smile, "Of course, I'd be happy to explain."

"When we set up a private limited company, we receive three important documents: the incorporation certificate, the Articles of Association (AOA), and the Memorandum of Association (MOA)," Vijay explained patiently. "These papers include something called authorised share capital. It means the total value of shares the company can issue. So, shares are like parts of this total value, and the founders can decide how to divide them."

Vijay was experienced, and these topics were his bread and butter. It was quite evident in how patiently he explained them. "As the company grows, you can decide how much the shares are worth based on factors like company assets, performance, profitability, growth, and industry scope. These factors help determine the company's value, which in turn finalises the price of its shares. There are complicated calculations involved in figuring out all this, but don't worry about them for now."

Vijay kept on explaining; however, it was too much for the trio. Anish slowly sat down on the floor while munching a samosa. All these new words were going over his head. Adi and Joy also struggled to understand, but they were determined to focus.

Vijay sensed the heaviness. He smiled and assured them, "Don't worry, guys. Starting a business doesn't require mastering all this information on day one. Remember, everyone learns as they go. Focus on your product and service offering; that's the most important thing for the business. The rest can be taken care of by experts. For now, Register the company first. You could even register from home or rent a coworking space."

One hour passed like a moment; Vijay had to leave due to other commitments, leaving the three engaged in a discussion about their next steps. "So, how do we proceed?" Joy inquired.

Anish proposed, "Let's start a business selling undergarments. We can rent a small store and start selling. It's low in investment, and we could avoid all the hassle of paperwork."

Adi, however, couldn't help but chuckle. "Come on, Anish, can't you dream bigger? Even a shop needs a trade licence and tax papers."

"Alright, Adi, your turn. What's your idea?" Joy prompted.

Adi grabbed a marker and approached the chart paper glued to the wall. "First, we need to establish a company with a trustable brand name. This brand will help us attract candidates."

Listening till here, Anish stood up to leave; Joy asked, "What's wrong?"

"I've had enough," Anish replied with a hint of bitterness. "We're broke. I've been smoking cheap cigarettes for the past 3 days for couple of bucks, and here, Gyani Baba dreams up grand schemes. I'm going to have my rum with peace; good night, guys."

Adi stopped Anish with a serious tone. "If you cannot dream, how will you make it?" He controlled his anger and lowered his voice, then softly started again, 'It's possible, Anish. Trust me, give me a chance to explain, please."

Anish stopped and softly signalled Adi to start."

"We'll register the company legally, but the rest will be smoke and mirrors. Additionally, we'll need to set up 2 separate companies," Adi explained, outlining his strategy.

"Two companies?" Joy and Anish exclaimed simultaneously; their surprise was evident.

"Yes, Two," confirmed Adi. "We need to differentiate between the recruitment company, which will handle payments, and the main company where employees will be recruited to work. This way, if any issues arise in the future, we can distinguish between the 2 entities."

"The recruitment company will operate as a training institute," Adi continued, brainstorming aloud. "It will take money from individuals and provide them access to a website to prepare for job exams for our main company. Let's give it a name."

"How about 'Soriya Digital'?" Joy suggested.

"That sounds fitting," Adi agreed. "Now, Soriya Digital will establish a partnership with another company. Let's name the training institute 'Anchor'."

"Anchor sounds good," Anish remarked.

"Indeed," Adi agreed. "So, Anchor will offer job opening options to individuals for a fee of 1500 rupees. In return, they'll gain access to 5 to 10 hours of course content to prepare for the job exam at Soriya Digital. As Anchor will collect the fees against the course content and job application, it will be a legitimate business transaction."

"But where will the course content come from? How will we obtain it?" Joy asked.

Anish responded confidently, "That's simple. We can create the material ourselves—basic software development concepts, along with IQ-related topics and all."

"Excellent, Anish. You're catching on," Adi praised him encouraged by their progress.

"So, what progress have we made so far?" Adi began, summarising the plan. "We've established Anchor, a company that will hunt for an entry-level software engineer position at Soriya Digital. Joy, you'll be in charge of developing the website where candidates can access the course content.

"Now, let's talk about Soriya Digital, the rock star of the show. We have to establish a strong online presence for this company as a major brand in the IT consulting field, and it may be headquartered in a foreign location. This company will partner with Anchor for recruitment solutions," Adi continued. "After one month of candidate registration with Anchor, Soriya Digital will conduct an exam and select 50 candidates to train as software engineers for the next year. This will be on-the-job training and fully paid."

"But will the training be effective? Can we train developers or testers from scratch in just one year?" Joy and Anish expressed their concerns.

"Many mass recruitment companies hire candidates from various engineering fields and train them in even less time," Adi responded.

"But they have infrastructure and trainers," Joy shared his concern.

"We'll have that too," Adi assured. "We'll rent an office space and set up basic infrastructure. Then, we'll hire a training company for the first 6 months of basic level training and the following 6 months of advanced training in coding, testing, infrastructure, and so on."

"But what about their fees?" Joy asked.

"Consider they will charge 50,000 rupees per head, that's a total of 25 lakhs for 50 candidates, while we'll have 15 crores sitting in the bank."

"Hmm, that sounds feasible," Joy and Anish nodded.

"But how will we create branding for Soriya Digital and even the global headquarters?" Anish inquired.

"Well, there will be no foreign headquarters for the company in real life. Joy, you will create a web presence for the company. Let's call it Cactus," Adi took a moment to name the company. "So, Cactus will be the parent company, and Soriya Digital will operate as a subsidiary of Cactus, which will be newly established in India.

"But how can we do that? It sounds impossible," Anish voiced his doubts.

"It's feasible," Joy insisted. "We can build a company over the Internet. Basically, a mirage."

"Yes, you're right, Joy. And Soriya Digital will be the shadow of the mirage," Adi added with excitement.

"But why do we need a foreign company?" Anish questioned.

"Because people trust imported things," Adi replied with a smile.

"I'm feeling dizzy now; I need a smoke," Anish said in his typical tone.

"Give me one too," said Adi. Joy also raised his hand for one.

They lit up their cigarettes; then Joy voiced his doubt, "But wait, won't the money go to Anchor's account instead of Soriya Digital?"

"Exactly," Adi confirmed with excitement. "Here's the game. After the first recruitment cycle, Anchor will acquire Soriya Digital. The merger of both companies will form our dream company, let's call it 'Soriya Digitech Pvt Ltd.' We will be founders of Anchor and eventually become the promoters of the merged entity, Soriya Digitech."

Anish surprisingly asked, "Then, who will be the founder of Soriya Digital?"

"Well, take a pause, guys," Adi said with a smile. "We need to find a ghost to represent Soriya Digital," Adi replied playfully. "After the merger, we will gradually phase out Cactus from the Internet over time."

Adi was lost in his vision; he could witness their company's foundation in front of his eyes. A founder needs to be able to see the vision with every minute detail and to feel every success and failure around it.

There is no doubt that Adi was a visionary; the business was like a child to him. And like a responsible father, he planned every detail of it.

At first, Adi, Joy, and Anish went from college to college, attempting to speak with students about job opportunities. However, most students either ignored them, suspecting it might be a scam or listened briefly before moving away. It didn't take long for them to feel hopeless.

One day, Anish said to Adi, "We have spent a lot, maxed out our credit cards, rented an office, created websites, registered the company, spent a lot on web branding and all, and here, no one is ready to even listen to us."

Joy also agreed, "Adi, this plan was easy on paper, but convincing this many people might not be easy. We are not selling government jobs."

Adi listened to them but was not yet out of hope. "Maybe our techniques are not correct," he said. "We are a country of 1.4 billion people, roughly 1 million graduates every year, everyone needs a job, but we cannot sell it?

How could it be possible? We must be missing something somewhere."

Adi asked Anish and Joy to hold all activities for a while and started building new strategies.

After spending a month in hibernation, Adi came up with a new plan. He called for a quick meeting.

"We were selling jobs, but people are not ready to buy them. Do you know why?" Adi asked.

"You tell," Anish replied, while Joy's expression remained similar.

"Okay," Adi continued, "Firstly, availability. People do not value things if they come too easily; they doubt it could be a scam. Secondly, trust. Candidates should learn about vacancies from a trusted source before searching for us. And thirdly, influence. We need to influence them with the right sources. In short, we need to create the market for our product"

"Okay, so you've analysed the problems well, but how will we solve this?" asked Joy.

Adi smiled and turned to Anish, "Do you have any questions too?"

Anish laughed and replied, "You will answer all our questions, I know. Please continue with your theory, Babaji."

Adi smiled and started again, "First, we still need to work a lot to build a strong brand. Our online branding is not sufficient. Start more intensive marketing. Also, arrange some tech seminars and invite techies to present there. Take photos and post them on social media. Create employee testimonies & Company reviews. Additionally, we have to create a narrative that Cactus is a well-established foreign-based company. Then, we'll start posting jobs for Soriya Digital, "A Cactus company," on all job portals. We'll interview applicants applying directly from job portals for a basic first round and push for the next round after payment."

Adi elaborated on his plan, "Next, we'll have to build good relations with college union leaders. We'll promote our offerings through them, which shouldn't be a problem with some financial incentives. We'll also need to build relations with placement cells and arrange seminars."

"Unions are fine, but will college authorities permit us to conduct seminars?" asked Anish.

Adi glanced at him and replied, "It's good that you asked, and even better, I already have a plan for that. We have a registered company now. Utilise it. We'll send letters to colleges and make cold calls to them. They'll have no reason to reject us, as we're trying to assist their students in getting a job. Our seminars will solely focus on corporate introductions and current market trends. We won't discuss our job openings. We'll simply establish a trusted reputation among the students."

Adi's plan worked. Over the next six months, the three of them travelled across India, conducting various seminars and building bonds with college unions. Some events went smoothly, while in others, they had to run to save their lives. However, their struggle ended when they reached their magic number of 1 lakh applications.

Adi's anticipation was correct; there were people struggling to get a good job. Some were even ready to pay bribes, while others spent on multiple coaching and courses. It was a market of hunger; all they needed to do was draw proper attention to the opportunity they were offering. Once they did it, the crowd chased after them.

Chapter 15

THE DOOMS DAY

Doomsday finally arrived, casting a shadow of uncertainty over the fate of Adi and Joy, along with their company and its 350 employees. Their destinies were to be decided today.

Adi wasn't able to sleep the entire night, eagerly waiting for the morning light. All his efforts and strategies would culminate in the outcome as the night passed. He didn't know what fate held for him, but he knew he had given it all he could.

As the first light of the sun started filtering through the curtains, signalling the start of the final battle, the persistent melody of the alarm clock echoed through the room. Adi's tired eyes remained fixed on the clock, showing no intention of silencing the bell or rousing him from his bed. Instead, he found himself lying in bed as if he lacked the strength in his body to wake up.

Today, Adi found himself without a plan, having exhausted all strategies. It was a day for waiting and watching, allowing destiny to write the final chapter. Despite his efforts to appear carefree, he was worried deep down, especially about Joy. So, he made a plan. He left his bed and began to write a confession on a notepad. Addressed to the honourable judge, accepting sole responsibility for all the actions and decisions of Soriya Digitech. He admitted his role, his lies, and his influence on others, clearing Joy and others of any blame.

As time passed, Adi found himself increasingly immersed in thoughts of uncertainty. Though he appeared calm on the outside, inside, he was grappling with questions and uncertainties about what to do. The path forward, once clear, now seemed hazy, like he was trying to see through thick fog.

Adi was a risk-taker. He had a strong belief in Murphy's Law, knowing that anything that could go wrong eventually would. With this mindset, he founded Soriya Digitech and carefully arranged each brick with a contingency plan in mind. And still, if it fails, Adi had the courage to face the consequences.

He signed the confession and kept it safe in his wallet; Adi felt a brief sense of relief. Though uncertain of what lay ahead, he found strength and a sense of comfort in facing his problems head-on and staying resilient despite challenges.

In the calm of the morning, it gave him a moment of peace, fleeting in the silence before the storm. Standing in front of the mirror, Adi observed himself closely. The reflection revealed a young man in pyjamas with messy hair and tired eyes. Despite his dishevelled appearance, he recognised a powerful man within himself. His strength and resilience stared back at him. With a smile, he patted his own shoulder and whispered words of encouragement, "Well done, Adi. You gave your best."

It was a moment of significance, a rare instance of self-affirmation. In life, we often seek validation from others, finding joy in their praise and feeling disheartened by their criticism. But Adi understands the importance of self-awareness. He believed there is no shame in being naked in front of the mirror, facing oneself honestly, and acknowledging both the strengths and flaws that God had gifted. To him, true success lies in recognising both strengths and weaknesses.

Adi knew that self-awareness was the key to unlocking life's mysteries and achieving success. By understanding his limitations, he gained the courage to plan and pursue his dreams. This self-awareness also empowered him to take ownership of his actions, forging his own path in life instead of following the crowd.

The doorbell rang, bringing Adi back from his thoughts. He made his way to the main door, where Tanya was waiting. She had returned with the early morning flight from her seminar, which was organised in Mumbai last evening. She rushed back to be by Adi's side on this crucial day. Tanya knew her role as Adi's source of calm in times of stress and how much he dependent on her presence to function properly.

Closing the door behind her, Tanya reached for Adi's hand, her touch offering reassurance. Drawing closer, she pressed her lips to his, knowing that he needed this moment of connection. Their kiss sparked a passionate exchange, and eventually, the couch in the hall became the arena for their embrace.

"Thanks for managing to come," Adi whispered gratefully.

"Don't thank me," Tanya replied softly. "You've always been there for me when I needed support."

Adi shared his stress about the day ahead, admitting that today he was without any backup plan.

"It'll be okay," Tanya reassured him. "At worst, they might shut down the company and fine you."

"But what if they send me to jail?" Adi's voice trembled with anxiety.

"You're worrying too much," Tanya replied, trying to ease his fears. "You have all the necessary paperwork, and you've also created jobs for so many people," she said optimistically. "Surely, the court will take that into account."

"Yeah, that's the last hope," Adi sighed, his faith wavering. "But I can't rely on destiny."

Tanya sensed Adi's inner turmoil, pulled him into a tight embrace, planting a gentle kiss on his lips. With a smile, she urged him to let go of his tension, reminding him that the outcome was out of their hands.

"No need to stress now," she whispered. "Let's just take a deep breath and have another round."

Adi smiled and surrendered himself in her arms.

The clock struck at 10, Adi prepared to leave for the court with Tanya by his side. But suddenly, something happened to Adi, and his behaviour changed. He took Tanya's hand in his, pulled her close, gently arranged her hair, and placed a tender kiss on her forehead. It was a side of Adi that Tanya had never seen before—romantic and deeply attached. Their relationship had always been strictly contractual, with no strings attached, as they always emphasised. But now, it seems different.

"What's wrong?" her voice trembled, touched by Adi's unusual behaviour. With a hint of mystery in his expression, Adi replied, "Perhaps today marks a new beginning for me."

He took a firm pause; a question lingered in the air. "If everything goes well today, will you..." He paused as his phone started ringing.

It was Joy calling. "Where are you?" Joy's voice was concerned.

"About to leave," Adi replied, puzzled. "Why?"

"Just wanted to make sure you're okay," Joy said. "Hurry up; I'll be waiting."

Before Adi could respond, Joy added, "No matter what happens today, remember that you're my best friend, and we're in this together."

Adi nodded silently before ending the call. His hand went to the confession letter tucked in his back pocket, but unconsciously, he decided to leave it there, lost in his thoughts.

Turning back to Tanya, Adi resumed, "If things go well today ..."

Tanya seemed to understand his unspoken words. Her eyes filled with tears. She found herself unable to hold back her emotions. "I will... Yes...I will ..." she whispered.

Adi held her tightly in his arms.

"I love you, Tani," he murmured, his voice filled with emotion. "I don't know when it happened, but now I can't imagine my life without you. Will you please marry me?"

Tanya tried to respond to Adi, but her voice choked with emotions, and tears flowed uncontrollably. She held Adi as tightly as possible as if trying to become one with him.

At that moment, something changed in her too. She realised how much she loved Adi and how deeply she wanted this relationship. Both of them hadn't realised when their casual encounters had grown so deep and intense.

Adi and Tanya rushed to the court, weaving through the large crowd gathered outside for the final verdict. The atmosphere was tense, with everyone eagerly awaiting the outcome of the case. The media and independent journalists were also present, capturing every detail of the unique scam.

Inside the courthouse corridor, they were surprised to see Joy with his family – Diya, Diya's mother, and his father. Adi felt a mix of surprise and nervousness at the unexpected sight of Joy's complete family.

Gathering his composure, Adi approached them with Tanya by his side. They respectfully touched the elders' feet, seeking blessings for the challenging journey ahead.

Diya's mother, who seemed warm and strong, cheered Adi. Her words were gentle and reassuring. You've been very brave and have faced many challenges already. Even if there are more ahead, don't lose hope. We're here for you and Joy; we will support both of you no matter what. she said, casting a glance at Joy.

Meanwhile, Joy's father held Adi and Joy's hands firmly, his voice filled with pride and hope. "I pray for your victory, my sons. May you succeed and bring honour to our family name. We eagerly await your return, proud and respected."

Adi and Joy were deeply moved by the kind words, their hearts filled with emotion. They exchanged a glance, silently acknowledging the significance of the moment. At that moment, Adi received a text message from his parents: "Good luck, my son. Do not get afraid; blessings from Ma and Baba are with you." A warm smile spread across Adi's face, strengthened by the blessings and support from his parents.

As someone once said, having family and loved ones by your side can lead to victory in any battle of life, while being without their support can lead to defeat, even in the simplest of challenges.

The courtroom proceedings started as per the schedule, with the public prosecutor delivering the opening argument. His tone was adamant as he presented a powerful case against Adi and Joy. The prosecutor showed video clips of interviews of the accused. He made it seem like the accused were trying hard to get public sympathy because they knew they had done wrong and were going to face consequences.

"These are just tricks," he said firmly, "typical of someone feeling guilty and trying to hide. Why else would they do such a public stunt?" The prosecutor's words carried a strong sense of belief as he criticised Soriya Digitech Pvt Ltd as a fake company run by dishonest people.

While listening to the prosecutor's condemnatory words, for a second, a seed of doubt took root in Adi's mind. Were they truly guilty of deception? Had they harmed innocent people in pursuit of their ambitions?

A heated argument between their lawyer, Mr Manjunath, and the public prosecutor pulled him back to reality within no time.

"Until the allegations are proven, you can't label my clients as criminals!" Manjunath thundered at the public prosecutor in court. The court sided with his argument.

The courtroom buzzed with the ongoing argument.

Manjunath argued, "Soriya Digitech Pvt Limited is a result of the merger between the former Soriya Digital Pvt Ltd and Anchor Pvt Ltd. My clients, Aditya Chowdhury and Joyabrata Ganguly, established a small recruitment & training company. Soriya Digital Pvt Ltd was their client."

He continued, "In the second year of its establishment, my clients acquired Soriya Digital in exchange for 50 lakh rupees and merged it with their company, Anchor, which formed today's Soriya Digitech Pvt Ltd."

The public prosecutor objected, "Well then, my dear friend, the court would like to know who was the owner or founder of the original Soriya Digital?"

Manjunath responded calmly, "Everything is documented. My dear PP sir, please review the case documents for clarification."

The public prosecutor, not ready to stop, continued, "Yes, my lord, according to the documents, a person named Gopal Majumder is listed as the founder of Soriya Digital. However, this person cannot be traced. I must inform the court that this individual does not even exist."

"I object, my lord," Manjunath roared. "All documents related to Gopal Majumder submitted to the court for review, along with his death certificate proving that he passed away naturally due to old age."

The argument took an interesting turn when it was proven that Adi and Joy were the founders of a legitimate company named Anchor Pvt Ltd. This company sold its courses and recruitment services to over 100,000 students, accumulating approximately 15 crores in its first season. With this capital, they acquired Soriya Digital from its founder, Gopal Majumder, leading to the formation of Soriya Digitech Pvt Ltd. This company annually recruited and deployed 50 candidates across various projects. It maintained meticulous paperwork, underwent yearly audits, and remained tax compliant.

Since its inception until last year, Soriya Digitech Pvt Ltd has even reported losses due to massive setbacks in the sales of its in-house digital products. The public prosecutor was not ready to spare Adi and Joy. He managed to access the company's initial days' sales and tax data, with which he claimed, "It was always a shell company, intended to cheat. The company, Soriya Digitech, never had a product or business. But it reported losses continuously for first three years. I want to ask my lord, what is going on here? A company without a business, reporting loss without any product?" his tone was sarcastic, but his attack was very strong, breaking the defence of Adi and Joy.

He continued, "These are all part of a well-planned scam. The company never had any business. To cover up the truth, they created another drama. Sorya Digitech acted well by selling basic open-source digital products levelled under their name. This drama was well-performed so that no one could question the company's business. And the fun part is they even enjoyed tax benefits due to the losses they recorded."

"Also, my lord," the PP continued, "Gopal Majumder never existed. These records confirming his natural demise are fake. I will request the honourable court to order a detailed investigation into Gopal Majumder."

Both sides presented their closing arguments, and the court adjourned for a break before delivering its final verdict.

Adi and Joy were waiting in the courtroom lobby, along with Tanya, Diya, and their families. Anish arrived with cups of tea for everyone, reassuring Adi, "Our defence is strong, Adi. Don't worry, unless they find Gopal Majumder, they have nothing against us."

Tanya, taken aback, repeated, "Us?" as she glanced at Anish with shock.

Adi nodded quietly, looking down.

Joy's father asked surprisingly, "I may not understand much about business, but initially, I believed Soriya Digitech was the company you both started. But listening to the whole story, I am confused. Just tell me one thing, have you two caused harm to anyone?"

Joy looked at his father, "Trust me, baba, your son would never harm anyone nor cheat a single penny from anyone."

The court resumed after the break; the suspense-filled the atmosphere as everyone awaited the judge's conclusions.

With a strong tone, He began, "As per the findings of this court, Aditya Chowdhury and Joyabrata Ganguly have engaged in legitimate business practices. They provided courses and recruitment services to deserving candidates, with 50 individuals successfully employed by Soriya Digitech Pvt Ltd each year. Over the last 4 years, a total of 200 candidates have been recruited. Furthermore, Soriya Digitech employs over 350 staff members who receive regular salaries and benefits. Therefore, the allegations of recruitment fraud and deceptive practices are groundless."

"Regarding the company's inception," the judge continued, "The claim of Late Gopal Majumder being the founder of Soriya Digital is proved, as all valid documents confirmed."

However, the court finds the act of influencing narratives via media involvement by the accused during the trial reprehensible and punishable. Therefore, the court orders the promoters of Soriya Digitech to refund ₹1500 examination fees to all candidates they have collected from, except those who have been employed. With that, the court releases Mr. Aditya Chowdhury and Joyabrata Ganguly from all other allegations, commending their efforts to generate employment for the youth."

EPILOGUE

Adi and Joy's victory wasn't just their own; it became a win for all the youths and those who dared to dream big. Their win was seen as a ray of innovation, igniting hope in millions from humble backgrounds with big visions. However, not everyone was pleased with that. Some intellectuals questioned the ethics and integrity of a businessman's victory, emphasising the importance of distinguishing between illegal and immoral actions. Some people saw the judgement as a fair ruling because the money taken from people was ordered to be returned, while the company was also allowed to continue growing.

The argument went online and on TV, with more and more people wanting to know about Gopal Majumder's past. Adi, who was used to handling such problems, took charge of the story and planned his next steps. They needed a good plan to calm the argument and get everyone to focus on their business again. So, they hurried to pay back all the money to the candidates, even with some basic interest.

Meanwhile Joy had concerns that giving back 1500 rupees to 4 lakh people would cost more than the company had, that even meant closing the company. But Adi already had a plan for this, even before the judgement; somehow, he anticipated this could happen and started working on the backup plan when Joy was in the hospital.

Berlin Equity Partners, one of the largest investment banks in the world, offered an investment deal in response to Adi's proposal. Now, they needed to finalise the deal by diluting some of their shares to obtain the necessary cash. This would enable them to return the money to the candidates, rebuild trust, and start fresh.

Adi and Joy resumed their regular office routine, finally experiencing peace of mind after a long hustle. Though they had a six-month timeline to repay the amount to the candidates, it seemed quite manageable compared to what they had just been through.

Adi called Joy into his cabin and briefed him on the ongoing investment discussions with BEP (Berlin Equity Partners), mentioning that they needed to prepare a strong pitch for this.

Eagerly, Joy inquired, "So, what's their offer, Adi?"

Adi explained, "They're willing to invest 150 crores for a 30 percent share in the company, valuing us at 500 crores INR."

"Wow, Adi, that's fantastic news!" exclaimed Joy.

Adi tempered the excitement, saying, "It's hopeful, Joy, but not quite fantastic yet. We need to convince them of our future plans and assure them of returns on their investment. Right now, their interest is just that – interest."

"When did all this happen?" Joy asked.

Adi smiled, "It was during your hospital stay. I received their initial reply. I had been working on this for some time. I've always had a plan to position the company for investment so that selling some of our shares could repay all the candidates I was about to discuss this with you, then all this legal drama started."

Joy queried further, "But how do you value our company at 500 crores? Isn't that more than our current standing?"

Adi explained, "It's simple. We had 10 crores in cash and 30 crores invested. We have 6 industry -leading clients with contracts spanning the next 6 years, plus 2 ready-to-launch products. So, asking for 500 crores isn't unreasonable."

Joy nodded, acknowledging the work ahead, "We have to work really hard on the pitch to secure this deal, Adi."

Adi agreed, "Yes, Joy, we need to seal the deal. Let's buckle up for Berlin."

"Berlin?!" Joy asked in shock.

"Yes, Berlin. BEP called us to their headquarters next month to present to their board."

"Wow, Let's do it," affirmed Joy as the previous charm returned to him. Adi could see a ray of sunshine in his friend after the dark night.

"But I have some action to take before boarding the flight to Berlin, Joy. I have to teach a lesson to someone who tried to stab us," Adi said with anger.

"Rajiv?" Joy asked.

"Yes, that guy needs a punch-back as a gift. Let me handle this. Meanwhile, please take care of the pitch. We will depart for Berlin on the 2nd of next month."

"All right, captain," said Joy with a big smile.

Adi and Joy were sitting on a chair outside of 'The Indian' restaurant in Kurfürstendamm, Berlin, smoking their favourite cigarette. Yesterday, they presented to the board of BEP, and today, they were called again for a final round of discussion. Both of them were very optimistic about receiving the check today. According to the court order, they only had a few months to pay back to the candidates. So, they were giving their best shot to close the deal and fulfil the court order. Once they pay back and close that chapter completely, they could freely move forward with their lives.

The restaurant was opposite their hotel. Both had prepared their pitches and were getting ready for further questions while sipping a cup of freshly brewed black coffee.

It was a pleasant spring morning in Berlin, the sun was smiling in the sky. the streets had transformed into a vibrant canvas with flowers blooming everywhere and fresh green leaves emerging on the trees after the dark winter. The air was filled with the sweet fragrance of flowers, mingling with the scent of coffee from cosy cafes tucked away in the corners.

This resonated with Adi and Joy's life. The long battle of the dark winter had ended with the court's verdict, offering some relief, yet they were still waiting for the warmth of the summer. Today's deal could finally bring the summer into their lives.

The old buildings with fancy designs stood silent across the street, witnessing the changing seasons. Their windows were decorated with flower boxes overflowing with colourful blooms. Walls covered in graffiti expressing the creative spirit of Berlin.

In spring, Berlin's streets weren't just paths from one place to another; they were like a stage for life. Every step was like a brushstroke on the city's soul.

Joy finished his cigarette and asked Adi, "Charlottenburg isn't far; should we take a walk?"

Adi smiled and replied, "It's always preferable to walk in this beautiful city."

They both started walking towards BEP's office.

Adi and Joy were sitting nervously in the waiting room next to the reception area. Suddenly, a well-built German gentleman came and invited them to the conference room.

Trying to impress the panel, Adi greeted them with a newly learned German phrase, "Guten Morgen" (good morning).

Alexander, the head of foreign investment, greeted them and delivered the bad news. "Gentlemen, we are willing to invest in your firm, but we disagree with the valuation. We believe your organisation should not be valued at more than 300 crores in INR."

This came as a shock to the duo. They tried to explain their calculations and the potential growth of the company, but the panel seemed unwilling to negotiate.

"It's our final offer, Mr. Aditya, Mr. Jayabrata. We won't mind if you decline. Please take your time and let us know your decision," said Alexander.

Adi sensed things were slipping away. Before he could say anything, Joy stepped in.

"Thank you for the offer, Mr. Alexander. You're offering based on our current business model, but we've always wanted to build a product for humanity, something that can save lives and make people feel less alone. We've never presented the product to anyone before. With your permission, I'd like to demonstrate our product to you. If you still think the valuation is correct after my presentation, we'll walk away."

Joy glanced at Adi, who nodded in agreement. It was the moment they'd been waiting for – a chance to present a product born from their hearts to a legitimate investor.

With enthusiasm, Joy began to explain their product – "a community-driven emergency service with features like ambulance services, online medicine, doctor consultations, Blood, or organ donation and so on. He described how users could build a community and seek help from each other in emergencies. They could connect for immediate help from the partnered services using the SOS button" Joy continued with full energy; no matter who was listening or liking the idea, all that mattered at that moment was that they finally had the platform to present.

As Joy finished his speech, the room erupted in applause. Alexander was impressed but had one question: "How will you make money?"

Adi jumped in as Joy made the stage for him, realising the idea had resonated with Alexander. He explained the various revenue models, including selling medical services, Health Insurance, ambulance, memberships, etc.

Alexander listened to them peacefully and had a small exchange with his colleague in German. He then turned to Adi and Joy and requested them to wait outside for some time.

Adi and Joy stepped out, overwhelmed. Something magical had happened in that room. They looked at each other, tears welling up, understanding each other without words. They hugged tightly, their journey flashing before their eyes – from struggling in the PG to this moment of recognition. Win or lose, doesn't matter, they had followed their dream, and that meant everything to these underdogs.

Suddenly, Alexander called them back in. Quickly wiping the tears, Adi and Joy re-entered the room.

"Congratulations, gentlemen. We agree to your proposal. You've got the deal.

Present days| *Three months later,*

Today is a memorable day for Adi and Joy. Their lives are changing from this moment; it is their wedding day. Both of them decided to marry on the same date so they can celebrate their anniversary together, forever. Adi and Tanya step into the next phase of life. They are still good friends and always will be, but they also realise that there is no harm in giving a name to their relationship.

Joy and Diya, on the other hand, feel fulfilled having each other. Diya knows Joy will hold her forever and will not leave her like her father.

Meanwhile, they received the investment and paid every individual with interest who had paid to them for the job application. The court order is fulfilled.

The marriage ceremony is organised in a farmhouse near Nandi Hills, Bangalore. Anish alone took charge of all the arrangements.

The weddings are arranged following Bengali traditions. Adi and Joy standing on the mandap as the brides arrive in a Palki, wearing red Banarasi saris and holding betel leaves to hide their faces. This is one of the cutest rituals of Bengali weddings, the Shubhodrishti. The bride hides her face with betel leaves and waits for the perfect moment to allow the groom to see her face. Friends and family hold a piece of cloth to create a shelter for them, and there, the first contact of their eyes as life partners takes place, creating a memorable bond for life.

Every aspect of a marriage ritual is meticulously crafted by the elders, each step serving as a psychological affirmation of one's new identity as a married individual.

It reminds them of the promises made to their life partner, cementing their commitment to each other for life. This is how two individuals from two different worlds become inseparable parts of each other.

After the rituals, the newlyweds join the guests on stage to receive blessings for their new life. Anish approaches and takes a photo with the couples. He congratulates them and hands over a gift box labelled 'from Gopal Majumder' with a mysterious smile.

He whispers in Adi's ear while leaving the stage, "Rajiv received his punishment. Both the defamation and sexual abuse cases at work were successful."

Adi responds with his usual mischievous smile. "Thank you, Gopal Majumder"

…..To be continued